A voice over th[e] ~~~ drew the gu[ard's]

Bolan watched as t[he] ~~~ [th]e message. Then, slow[ly] ~~~ Executioner, his smi[le] ~~~ ~~~atchy radio voice raved on as the ~~~[rd]'s hand moved casually toward the flap of his holster.

Had he spoken fluent Turkish, Bolan couldn't have understood the radio message more clearly. He floored the Fiat's accelerator. The tiny engine sputtered, then caught, jerking him back against the seat as the Turk's gun cleared leather.

The warrior was halfway to the Syrian checkpoint before the Arab guard realized what was happening. The man took a step back from the roadway, drew his revolver and waited as the Fiat neared.

Bolan watched him sight in as his target came into range. He ground the stick shift into third as the man fired, the Fiat jerking and whining as the bullet ricocheted harmlessly off the pavement. Gunning the engine, the warrior returned the car into fourth and sailed past into Syria.

In the rearview mirror, Bolan saw a Turkish jeep racing down the road toward the Syrian station. He reached over his shoulder, securing the seat belt and the harness around him. The chase had only begun.

MACK BOLAN®

The Executioner

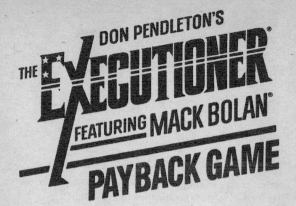

DON PENDLETON'S
THE EXECUTIONER®
FEATURING MACK BOLAN®

PAYBACK GAME

A GOLD EAGLE BOOK FROM
WORLDWIDE.

TORONTO • NEW YORK • LONDON • PARIS
AMSTERDAM • STOCKHOLM • HAMBURG
ATHENS • MILAN • TOKYO • SYDNEY

First edition March 1991

ISBN 0-373-61147-1

Special thanks and acknowledgment to
Jerry VanCook for his contribution to this work.

PAYBACK GAME

The life of humanity upon this planet may yet come to an end, and a very terrible end. But I would have you notice that this end is threatened in our time not by anything that the universe may do to us, but only by what man may do to himself.

—John Haynes Holmes
1879–1964

We have no control over what the universe throws at us—we accept it and deal with it. But if mankind intends to stand back and tolerate the horrors some men inflict on other men, count me out. I'll fight back every time.

—Mack Bolan

THE
MACK BOLAN®
LEGEND

Nothing less than a war could have fashioned the destiny of the man called Mack Bolan. Bolan earned the Executioner title in the jungle hell of Vietnam.

But this soldier also wore another name—Sergeant Mercy. He was so tagged because of the compassion he showed to wounded comrades-in-arms and Vietnamese civilians.

Mack Bolan's second tour of duty ended prematurely when he was given emergency leave to return home and bury his family, victims of the Mob. Then he declared a one-man war against the Mafia.

He confronted the Families head-on from coast to coast, and soon a hope of victory began to appear. But Bolan had broken society's every rule. That same society started gunning for this elusive warrior—to no avail.

So Bolan was offered amnesty to work within the system against terrorism. This time, as an employee of Uncle Sam, Bolan became Colonel John Phoenix. With a command center at Stony Man Farm in Virginia, he and his new allies—Able Team and Phoenix Force—waged relentless war on a new adversary: the KGB.

But when his one true love, April Rose, died at the hands of the Soviet terror machine, Bolan severed all ties with Establishment authority.

Now, after a lengthy lone-wolf struggle and much soul-searching, the Executioner has agreed to enter an "arm's-length" alliance with his government once more, reserving the right to pursue personal missions in his Everlasting War.

PROLOGUE

The familiar wave of terror, stark and all-encompassing, flooded the woman's being as the hood descended over her eyes. She prayed, willing herself not to think about what might happen...was *going* to happen.

She felt a sharp pain in her earlobe, then an earring clattered to the floor as coarse hands gripped her shoulders and dragged her from the mattress. She recoiled and shuddered when her captors' hands made contact with her skin. From both sides she heard soft moans as the others were pulled to their feet.

The woman heard the rip of adhesive tape and felt the cool stickiness on her wrists. More hands led her to the door before whirling her through a seemingly endless series of spins. She grew light-headed.

"You don't need to—" the woman started to say.

"Don't speak!" a voice commanded.

She continued spinning, the hands moving from shoulder to shoulder as if turning a wheel. Nausea rose from her stomach to her throat. The rotations finally stopped, and the woman heard low, guttural laughter as she fought to regain equilibrium.

Slowly the hands slid from her shoulders to her breasts, kneading the soft flesh beneath the thin pajama top. Then one hand trailed down her stomach, stopping between her thighs. The nausea returned as her captor's breath quickened. The sickening odors of curry and dates blended to assault her face. She felt the hand on her breast move to the waistband of her pajamas.

Instinctively she squeezed her thighs together.

Harsh words in the foreign tongue came from over her shoulder. The woman sensed movement to her side and heard a sharp slap directly in front of her. The hands dropped.

Angry voices argued momentarily, then a softer grip led her up the stairs and out into the night. Dry heat blasted the woman's face, and she felt sweat break out on her upper lip. An engine hummed, and she heard the metallic sounds of a sliding door. The hands lifted her.

The woman stumbled and fell to the floor as more bodies were pressed through the opening. As the vehicle drove through the night, the woman heard sporadic gunfire in the distance. In the intervals of silence, she fantasized about being rescued. But it would never happen.

The woman's head snapped forward as they jerked to a stop. Salty sea air stung her nostrils as the door slid open and she was pulled from the van.

The woman felt the deck roll under her as she settled in the boat. A motor kicked to life, then currents of watery wind blasted against the hood as the craft streaked through the night. Droplets of water rolled down the canvas, soaking through the pajamas to raise goose bumps on her skin.

Suddenly the wind died, and the temperature dropped. The woman shivered as hands lifted her over the side, depositing her in another, rocking seat. Another motor started, softer this time, and she heard the sound echoing faintly off nearby walls. Then someone killed the motor and the boat glided silently to a halt.

Once more hands lifted the woman, pushing her to a sitting position on a cold stone floor. The hood was removed and the woman squinted painfully as her eyes struggled to focus in the light.

Seated around her were eight bound forms. Where were the others? There had been sixteen of them in the basement.

In the center of the cavern the woman saw a high wooden platform. Directly in front of her, one of her captors stood behind a tripod-mounted video camera.

The woman watched as her captors whispered among themselves before dragging one of the hostages up the steps. It was then that she noticed the rope dangling from the platform.

The leader barked instructions from below as they slipped the noose around the hostage's neck. She saw the man look down, his eyes coming to rest on her. He smiled grimly.

The woman screamed and was rewarded with a slap to the face. The leader spoke softly into the camera. Among the strange-sounding words, the woman made out "Presidents" and "Satan" and "Allah." Then the camera turned toward the platform and U.S. Army Major Randolph Groethe dropped to his death.

A strange dullness clouded her brain. As if from far away, the woman felt the hands as they pulled her to her feet. The leader's arm encircled her shoulders, yanking her in front of the camera. He pressed a long-bladed knife to her throat. The woman heard her name.

"One week!" the wild-eyed man screamed as he shook his fist at the camera.

The woman was thrown back onto the floor. The hood slid down once more, returning her to the darkness.

1

The man with the wiry black beard had been careless, and that carelessness would cost him his life.

Keeping one eye on the man across the aisle, Mack Bolan sipped from the plastic highball glass. Moments before, the warrior had seen a glint of blue steel under the sport coat as the man twisted in his seat to accept the tray from the flight attendant. That quick glimpse had confirmed the Executioner's suspicions. The man with the beard was Ali Hammami, a member of the Islamic terrorist group Al Dawa.

The Executioner hadn't wasted time wondering how the weapon had crossed security. The possibilities were only limited by the imagination, and each was irrelevant at this point. What mattered was that the gun *was* on board.

Bolan had watched Hammami's movements since boarding the plane, noting the furtive glances and nods he periodically gave the man at the front of the cabin. He wondered how long it would be before the two made their move.

Battle-seasoned instincts told the Executioner that they'd wait—at least for a while. Lufthansa Flight 414 wasn't yet halfway from Paris to Ankara. Darkness would soon fall over the plane, and many of the passengers would take advantage of the opportunity to sleep.

Hijackings that failed usually failed in the first few moments—before the takeover could be established—and a planeload of half-groggy passengers would be less likely to resist.

The Executioner had planned to catch a quick nap himself, but those plans had changed. Bolan leaned back against the seat, positioning himself so that he could watch both men, unnoticed. There were no more quick glances. The Al Dawa men now studiously avoided each other's eyes.

The Executioner glanced at his watch. He could wait, too. For a while.

His mind drifted back over the lightning-fast events of the past eighteen hours. He'd set up base in a Detroit hotel room across the street from Polly's Paradise, the preferred night spot of Val Santino. Bolan had stalked the mafioso triggerman for days, carefully selecting the right time and place to surgically remove yet another of society's cancerous growths.

He'd been making final preparations to send a bullet through the hit man's skull when television news broke the story.

"Retaliating for the kidnapping last Friday of spiritual leader Sheikh al-Sadr by Israeli forces, Hizbullah terrorists have executed U.S. Army Major Randolph Groethe," the newswoman read over the air. "Hizbullah is demanding the sheikh's immediate return, as well as the release of thirty-seven convicted terrorists currently imprisoned in Israel. The terrorists have threatened to execute one hostage per week until their demands are met."

The network had run the videotape of Groethe's execution. The death appeared real—it was there in living color on the six o'clock news.

Bolan returned his attention to the man across the aisle. Hammami picked nervously at his meal.

While Al Dawa had links to Hizbullah, the two Shiite terrorist factions were separate. The hijacking about to be attempted wasn't likely to be directly related to the American hostage situation.

A small piece of meat fell from Hammami's fork onto his lapel. He glanced around the cabin before dabbing the spot with a napkin.

Bolan relaxed again. They weren't ready. Not yet.

His thoughts returned to the hotel room. With several hours before Val Santino would arrive at the club, Bolan had placed an emergency call to Hal Brognola.

"It's real, all right," the Justice man had confirmed.

"Call Grimaldi," Bolan had told him. "Tell him to grab a plane and meet me—"

Brognola's uneasy cough had stopped the Executioner. "There's more to it, Striker."

In the next few minutes Bolan learned the story that would never hit the news. The President was engaging in secret negotiations with the Iranian government. The new regime in Tehran seemed cooperative and eager to help in the quick location and return of the sixteen Americans who'd been held hostage for over two years.

Nothing that might endanger this new relationship between Washington and Tehran was to be attempted. Under no circumstances was any covert action to take place. The orders came straight from the White House.

Brognola had coughed again. "The Man sent special notice to *you,* Striker."

"There's no way they can pull it off, Hal," Bolan remembered telling him. "Too many variables. Israel's demands may coincide with ours in part, but by the time they've ironed out the details, the hostages will all be dead."

"No argument here," Brognola had agreed. "We tell the world we won't negotiate with terrorists. Then we turn around and say we'll talk to anyone, do anything, to get them back safely. I'm confused as hell as to what our policy really is. If we even have a policy." Brognola went on to offer his services "behind the scenes." Aaron Kurtzman at Stony Man Farm had agreed to aid the Executioner in violation of the orders, as well.

But Bolan could never allow old friends to place themselves in such jeopardy. The Executioner would take this one alone. All alone.

Across the aisle Hammami handed his tray to the flight attendant and folded the table into the seat in front of him. He rose slowly, carefully holding his coat to his side, and walked down the aisle to the rest room.

Bolan's mind returned to the newscast. The videotape had shown the raving, savage-eyed leader of Hizbullah holding a knife to the throat of Sharon Walker. The American woman would be the next to die. She had six days left.

Unless the Executioner got to her first.

The urgency of the situation had left Bolan with no time to plan and execute a scheme to bring weapons through French and Turkish customs. Unarmed, he had grabbed the passport and the rest of his "Mike McKay" identification and boarded the first flight from Detroit to New York. TWA had gotten him to Paris, where he'd hooked into the German airline to Turkey.

The McKay identity had been created by Kurtzman at Stony Man. "McKay" was a quick-tempered, hard-drinking free-lance writer with ties to no one. The freedom that life-style provided had proved handy to Bolan in the past.

Bolan ordered a Scotch, pocketing the miniature bottle as soon as the stewardess was out of sight. He leaned back in the seat and watched through half-opened eyes as Hammami returned, opened the overhead compartment and took out a pillow. Five minutes later the pilot dimmed the cabin lights, and the passengers' voices faded to whispers.

Bolan unknotted his necktie and folded it into the side pocket of his sport coat. He quickly scanned the darkened cabin. The flight was only half-full, and most of the weary travelers had adjusted their seats and turned off the overhead lights. The rest sat quietly reading or whispering among themselves.

Bolan rose casually and moved to the empty seat behind Hammami, pulling his tie from his pocket as he went. Making one last glance throughout the plane, he leaned forward and looped the tie around the terrorist's neck.

With a sudden jerk Bolan pulled up and back with both hands, tightening the makeshift garrote against the man's throat. Hammami struggled briefly, then his body went limp.

Stuffing the tie back into his pocket, the Executioner moved quickly around the seat. He repositioned the terrorist's head on the pillow and pulled a Glock 17 automatic from the man's belt before returning to his seat across the aisle.

The man's death wouldn't be discovered until the flight ended, and it would be presumed that he'd died in his sleep. The bruises on his neck were faint from the soft silk tie, and even that scanty evidence would be camouflaged by the hair of his beard. Until an autopsy could be performed, the cause of death would remain uncertain. And by then the Executioner would be through Turkish customs and headed toward Syria.

Bolan glanced toward the front of the plane to where Hammami's partner was reading the airline flight magazine. The other man presented a problem. Two deaths on the same flight would be too much of a coincidence to be ignored.

Bolan rose once more and walked to the front of the cabin, smiling as he approached the blond flight attendant. "Any chance of getting a beer to chase down the Scotch?"

The woman eyed him briefly, then returned the smile. "Certainly, sir." She turned, reached into the refrigerator and uncapped a chilled bottle of Grolsch before handing it to him.

"Thanks."

The next move had to be perfect. The Executioner needed to accomplish his objective without drawing the attention of the rest of the passengers.

Two rows from where the second terrorist sat, Bolan stubbed his foot and lurched forward, catching himself on the seat in front of the man. Beer sloshed forward out of the upturned bottle, the foam flying onto the terrorist's trousers. The man looked up, muttering under his breath.

Bolan tightened his abdominal muscles, forcing blood to his face as if embarrassed. "Shorry," he slurred, and returned to his seat.

Watching from the rear, he saw the terrorist wiping at the mess with a small cocktail napkin. With a frustrated look on his face, the man stood and walked toward the tail of the plane.

The Executioner let him pass, then got up and followed him down the aisle. As the man opened the rest room door, Bolan pushed him through and slipped in behind.

The terrorist started to turn, his face a combination of surprise, fear and hatred. Bolan reached up with both hands, grabbing his chin and hair.

The Executioner caught the man around the neck with a forearm, crushing the radial bone of his wrist into the terrorist's windpipe. Pushing hard against the back of the man's head with the other arm, he squeezed until the man lost consciousness.

The warrior pulled the small Scotch bottle from his pocket and sprinkled half of it over the limp form. The rest room took on the odor of a Bowery tavern.

Pouring the rest of the liquor into the terrorist's open mouth, he reached under the man's coat to find an Ingram M-11 hanging from a shoulder sling. Removing the magazine and opening the bolt, he quickly emptied the weapon.

Bolan draped an arm over his shoulder and carried the terrorist down the aisle. The flight attendant approached as he lowered the man into his seat.

"What's wrong?" she asked.

"Drinking too much."

Her eyebrows rose. "He's your friend?"

Bolan shrugged. "Just met him on the flight."

"But he refused when I offered cocktails. I thought he must be Muslim and didn't indulge."

"Probably *is*," Bolan replied. He reached into the terrorist's coat pocket and produced the empty Scotch bottle. "That's why he hides it."

The flight attendant nodded and returned to her seat.

It was time to face the next problem.

While there were countless ways to smuggle weapons on board commercial flights, they all fell into two basic categories. The terrorists had either boarded the plane armed, or the guns had been waiting for them. Either way, it meant a third party was involved in the hijacking attempt.

Bolan looked up the aisle to where the flight attendant sat, filing her nails with an emery board. In all likelihood that third party was a member of the crew.

THE AL DAWA GUNMAN rested peacefully throughout the remainder of the night, starting to regain consciousness just as Flight 414 began its descent over Ankara.

Bolan glanced around, assured himself there were no curious eyes, then "rocked" the terrorist back to sleep.

Shifting slightly, the Executioner felt the hard steel and plastic of the Glock against his back. He faced a decision. He needed to obtain armament for whatever battles lay ahead in his quest to free the hostages, and the high firepower that the Glock provided could prove invaluable.

But keeping it meant risking discovery by customs officials upon entry into the country. Turkish customs were usually lax about checking incoming flights. But anything could happen, and should officials decide on a spot check at this point, it would mean a Turkish prison for the Executioner. And death for the hostages.

Bolan glanced once more to where the flight attendant sat. If she represented the "third party" in the unsuccessful hijacking, she wouldn't likely risk discovery by blowing the whistle.

But if the pretty blonde had no involvement, she might find the Ingram on the sleeping terrorist after the rest of the passengers deplaned and alert customs before the Executioner had passed through.

As so many times before, over the countless years of combat, Bolan faced a calculated risk. He'd take it and play it by ear.

As the wheels hit the runway, the Executioner made a final check of the Al Dawa man, carefully positioning the unconscious form so that the machine pistol didn't show.

Having checked no luggage through, Bolan grabbed his carryon, deplaned and proceeded through the Ankara airport toward customs. The terminal bustled with activity as he made his way along the concourse. Moving casually through the cafés and shops selling meerschaum pipes, brass ware and local crafts, he passed a mailbox, then stepped into an empty rest room.

Bolan took a place at the urinal. He had no desire to be the first person scrutinized in the customs line. A minute later he left the rest room and took a place at the end of the line, watching as a uniformed Turk stamped passports and scratched Xs on the suitcases with a piece of white chalk.

He stood fourth in line when the blond flight attendant came racing down the concourse. In the middle of the German-accented Turkish that poured from her mouth, Bolan caught the word *machine gun* and saw the uniformed men straighten.

Casually he stepped out of line. Keeping his pace moderate, he walked back toward the rest room.

In the distance he saw a tourist group of three dozen Orientals laughing and chattering in front of the rest room. Then, from behind, came a shrill whistle and a voice cried *"Dur!"* Bolan quickened his step.

Merging with the boisterous Japanese, he maneuvered toward the mailbox, hoping the group would conceal his movements. Reaching the mailbox and without breaking stride, Bolan pulled the Glock from his waistband and dropped it through the slot, then continued on into the rest room.

Moving directly to a toilet stall, he lifted the bowl lid and flushed. He'd just turned back toward the door and was fumbling with his belt when two customs officers burst into the room, guns drawn.

Bolan raised his hands in surprise as both men screamed orders in Turkish. Moving cautiously forward, the taller of the two men, slightly overweight and with a small pencil mustache, ran one hand around the Executioner's belt line, then up and down his legs. The other hand pressed a 9 mm pistol into the Executioner's midsection.

"Why you leave line?" the man demanded in broken English.

Bolan glanced over his shoulder at the toilet stall, then grimaced and pointed toward his stomach.

The customs man looked up into his eyes, his face a mask of disbelief. The other officer said something and indicated the toilet. He pushed the Executioner aside and strode into the stall. The toilet was still gurgling. Scowling, he turned back and demanded, "Passport."

Bolan reached inside his sport coat.

The man with the mustache studied the document, looking first at Bolan, then the picture, then back at Bolan. "You are ... writer, Mr. McKay?"

"Yes."

"What is your ... company?"

"I'm free lance," Bolan told him. The puzzled look he got made it obvious the man didn't understand. "I work for myself."

The customs officer frowned. "How you find work?" he asked.

Bolan shrugged. "It finds me."

The customs man held the passport in front of him. "I am not so sure to believe you, Mr. McKay. Where you will stay in Ankara?"

Bolan looked the man in the eye. "Buyuk Ankara."

The man's eyebrows rose slightly. The Buyuk was one of Ankara's two deluxe-rated hotels. "Ah," he said skeptically. "You have ... how you say ... reserves?"

"Reservations," Bolan corrected him. "And, yes. You can check."

"We will do this thing. Not to leave Ankara. We call you at Buyuk tomorrow. Not to leave."

Bolan nodded and replaced the passport. By tomorrow he'd be in Syria.

The two customs officers escorted Bolan from the rest room back to the line. The tall man with the mustache stamped his passport and waved him through. "We call tomorrow," he repeated. "Not to leave. This thing is...orders."

Bolan shouldered his carryon and walked to the nearest exit. Stepping out onto the streets of the Turkish capital, he filled his lungs with the thin air of the Anatolian Plateau.

Orders. During his years in the Army, the Executioner had almost always obeyed orders. Since he'd left the Army, things had changed.

"ANYTHING TO GET ME started?"

"Not much, Striker. A name and a town—Hossein, a rug dealer in Antioch. He's been with the Company for about six months. Supposed to know someone who knows someone who knows someone."

"Hossein who sells rugs in Antioch? You've got to be kidding. Is that all?"

"Sorry. Call me when you get to Turkey. Maybe—"

"Forget it, Hal. You're getting close to the end of a thin limb already. Thanks."

The sudden buzz of the alarm clock roused Bolan from a dream in which he'd been replaying his last conversation with Brognola. Shaking the cobwebs from his head, he sat up on the bed.

His eyes fell on the watch on the nightstand—0215 hours. He had just enough time to shave, shower and make it back to the airport before the flight south to Adana left the ground.

Twisting the shower knob, Bolan let the cold water shock him into full consciousness. His mind reflected on the dream. So far he'd been too busy stopping hijackings and avoiding Turkish prisons to come to terms with the real problem of the mission: where did he start? He had next to nothing to go on.

Bolan killed the water, stepped from the shower and grabbed a towel from the rack. He walked, dripping, into the bedroom as he dried his hair.

The Executioner shook his head. Hossein in Antioch who sold rugs. It was like finding the proverbial needle in the haystack. It could be done all right, but it would take time. And time was the one thing he was short of.

A quick image of Sharon Walker filled his mind. The woman stood before the video camera, her eyes wide in terror as the edge of the terrorist's blade pressed into her throat. Time was what she, too, lacked most.

Bolan folded his suit and dropped it into the carryon. He slipped a short-sleeved pullover shirt over his head and tucked it into khaki slacks. The outfit provided no concealment for weapons.

Digging into his carryon, Bolan lifted the shallow false bottom and retrieved a small brown envelope. Straightening the metal tabs, he opened the flap and pulled out a passport. He stuffed the Mike McKay identification into the envelope and replaced it at the bottom of the bag.

Mack Bolan became Pat Harding.

Halfway to the hotel, he'd stopped the cab. A quick call to the Buyuk had revealed that, yes, he had already received a call.

There was only one person who knew where he was staying. The customs official was checking out his story.

Assuring the desk clerk he'd check in later, the Executioner had hung up, calling again a few minutes later to secure a room under the Harding name. Shortly after arriving at the Buyuk, he'd phoned in a second reservation on the flight to Adana. Both McKay and Harding were now booked on the flight.

That provided him with two possible IDs for the flight south. Both had advantages—both had potential problems. He'd play it by ear.

The Ankara-Adana flight was domestic, so it wasn't likely that there'd be a passport check. Bolan hoped not. It would be safer boarding the flight as Harding, but there was no record of a Patrick Harding having entered Turkey.

On the street in front of the hotel Bolan hailed a cab. Traffic moved smoothly along the tree-lined avenues as they passed the modern architecture of Ankara. Occasionally the steel and glass was broken by the spires of an ancient mosque. Bolan gazed out the window. For a city founded thirty centuries ago, little remained of the past.

Bolan paid the cabbie and blended into a British tour group as he entered the terminal. He made his way toward the Turkish Airlines ticket counter.

The dark-skinned young man behind the counter wore the navy blue jacket of the airline. He issued Bolan a ticket and boarding pass. "Concourse Four," he said in flawless English. "Gate Seventeen."

Bolan nodded.

A party of German men passed the ticket counter as Bolan turned. The Executioner fell in behind them, exchanging brief smiles with the men.

They'd just turned a corner and were twenty yards from the entrance to Concourse Four when Bolan spotted the customs officer. The man with the pencil mustache leaned against the wall next to a coffee shop, grinning ear to ear as he spoke animatedly to a large-busted flight attendant. He looked up as the group approached.

Falling a half step behind, Bolan used the Germans to shield his face, then turned into a kiosk selling tobacco and candy.

The Executioner watched in the reflection of the glass behind the counter as he examined the tobacco in front of him. The customs official gave his back a reflexive once-over, then returned his eyes to the woman at his side.

Bolan purchased a newspaper, then took a seat in the waiting area, holding the newspaper in front of his face. He ignored the first boarding call. If discovery came, he preferred it be in the terminal where he could maneuver, not within the confines of a Boeing 727.

When the last call finally came, the warrior folded the newspaper and pulled the boarding pass from his carryon, handing it to the flight attendant at the entrance to the ramp. The woman glanced up. "American?" she asked.

Bolan nodded and started to pass.

"Stop."

He paused, looking down.

"Must check the passport . . . for foreigner." She smiled.

The Executioner hesitated. It couldn't be routine procedure. He'd seen the Germans, as well as an Oriental couple, board before him.

There had to be some other reason that the flight attendant wanted his identification. If he handed her the Harding ID, she was bound to notice that it hadn't been stamped. But if he gave her McKay, and she'd been notified to look out for that name. . . .

Bolan smiled down at the woman as he reached into the carryon, flipped up the false bottom inside the bag and pulled out the brown envelope.

She glanced quickly at the picture, then blushed and lowered her head in embarrassment. "My name is Mozgan," she said shyly. "I will be on your flight, Mr. McKay." She raised her eyes cautiously. "I am, too—how do you say in English—forward?"

Bolan felt the muscles in his neck relax. "Not at all, Mozgan. Call me Mike."

The woman's face broke into a smile, her full lips opening to show a row of perfect snow-white teeth. "I will see you on board . . . Mike."

2

The capital of Adana Province bustled with activity as Bolan pulled the Fiat away from the rental office. Passing the age-old white Akca Mosque, he made his way toward the south edge of the city of Adana.

The flight from Ankara had been uneventful, and the Executioner would have liked to have taken advantage of the opportunity and grabbed another short nap. But Mozgan had had other plans.

As soon as the ice had been broken at the ramp entrance, the sloe-eyed Turkish beauty had become a nonstop scattergun of conversation. Slipping into the seat next to him, she'd run down her entire biography. At least Bolan assumed that she had. If anything had been left out, he couldn't imagine what it might be.

When she'd finally been forced out of her seat to prepare for landing, Mozgan had crammed a slip of paper with her phone number and address into Bolan's hand.

"You will...call me?" she'd asked.

"Sorry," Bolan had told her. "There's another woman waiting for me."

And Bolan was thinking of Sharon Walker.

The Executioner turned the Fiat onto Highway E-5 toward the ancient Hittite settlement of Misis. He felt himself shaking his head in frustration.

Hossein who sells rugs in Antioch.

Bolan pushed the futility from his mind. Defeatist thoughts had never been part of the Executioner's psyche. He hadn't survived the countless battles fought over the years by allowing pessimism to gain a foothold in his mind. It had always been an affirmative nature, combined with the combat skills mastered on fields of fire the world over, that had allowed him to emerge victorious where other men failed.

At Toprakkale the E-5 branched south and the Fiat kept a steady pace as it crossed the Plain of Issos. Periodically Bolan spot-checked the speedometer, careful not to let his speed rise more than ten kilometers over the posted limit. Time was of the essence, but detainment by Turkish police would consume more of that diminishing commodity than slower speed.

Densely wooded mountains forced the highway closer to the coast near Alexandretta. Bolan considered the next rung of the ladder he had to climb to find the hostages.

Hossein who sells rugs in Antioch.

Antioch had a population of roughly one hundred thousand people. The warrior had no idea how many places sold carpets, or how many salesmen were employed in the process. But there had to be plenty. And more than a few would be named Hossein.

He hadn't wanted to press Brognola, aware that his old friend's neck already rested on the chopping block. But Bolan had sensed that the tip about Hossein had come in passing—it was something the Justice man had picked up by accident and was never meant to know. That meant it could be accurate, altered or totally false.

The CIA's contact could be a retailer, a wholesaler or an importer. The right Hossein might be an executive in a large rug distributorship or a merchant hawking his wares at a kiosk on the streets. The right Hossein might very well be a smuggler keeping a low profile, in which case it could take days or weeks to run him down.

Days or weeks the Executioner, Sharon Walker and the other hostages didn't have.

But it was all he had. And he had to start somewhere.

Bolan crested a hill and saw the ancient city in the distance. Pressing slightly on the accelerator, he increased his speed until the outline of modern apartment buildings became visible. The Executioner passed through the residential area, nearing Antioch's Oriental core.

As he turned onto a quiet tree-lined street, a light drizzle began to fall. Bolan had just switched on the windshield wipers when a hotel appeared in the distance.

Turning the Fiat into the parking lot, he pulled the keys from the ignition and entered the lobby. The short, squat man behind the desk was lighting the end of one acrid-smelling cigarette with the stub of another. Above the scarred wooden counter Bolan saw that the man wore an American Izod shirt. The top of his black slacks curled downward, losing the battle they fought against the roll of fat at his waist. He looked up as Bolan crossed the threshold, then turned back to his cigarette. Satisfied, his eyes returned to Bolan.

"*Evet?*" he asked.

"English?" Bolan returned.

A grin covered the fleshy face. "Yes. What can I do for you?"

"I'm looking for a friend. My Turkish is a little rusty."

"You staying the night?" the desk clerk asked.

"No. I just need help."

"*Ozur dilerum* . . . excuse me. My English is getting rusty."

The warrior pulled a roll of Turkish liras from his pocket and peeled off two large-denomination bills.

"It's getting better," the clerk said. He raised his hand, palm up, and wiggled his pudgy fingers.

Bolan handed him two more bills and watched them disappear into his pocket.

"Ah, my English is completely restored." The man smiled. "Now, how can I help?"

"I'm looking for a man named Hossein who sells rugs somewhere in Antioch."

The desk clerk looked at Bolan skeptically. "Did I hear you correctly?"

"I'm afraid so."

The man shook his head. He reached under the counter and set a phone book on the desk between them. "We must not overlook the obvious," he said. "Who knows. You might get lucky."

The desk clerk thumbed through the book. "Ah, sometimes you *do* get lucky." He turned the book toward Bolan and pointed at the page with a stubby finger. "The English equivalent is Hossein's Carpet Sales." He beamed. "Is this your friend?"

Bolan shrugged. "Could be." He tossed another bill onto the counter.

The desk clerk tore a slip of paper from a pad by the phone and wrote the address and directions in English.

"Thanks," Bolan said and left.

Sometimes you *did* get lucky.

But there were still a lot of variables in the game. Just because Hossein was in the book didn't mean he was the CIA informant.

Hossein's Carpet Sales sat at the center of a block of two-story buildings on the edge of the downtown shopping district. Bolan drove by once, surprised to see the shop front darkened and a sign in the window that he presumed meant Closed. The rest of the street boomed with activity as customers and street vendors haggled over the prices of the merchandise offered for sale.

Bolan parked the Fiat up the street, locked the doors and walked back to the shop. Hand above his eyes to block out the sun, the Executioner peered into the darkened window.

Overlapping stacks of Oriental carpets littered the display room. At the far end Bolan could make out the obscure outline of an antique cash register atop a counter. Behind the counter faint light glowed through a partially open door. He glanced at his watch.

He had no way of knowing if this Hossein was the right man, and he couldn't afford to waste valuable time waiting. It made more sense to find another lead—another Hossein to run down—and return later when the shop opened.

Bolan turned to leave, then heard a muffled cry from inside the shop. Moving instinctively away from the window, he pressed his ear against the cracked paint of the door.

Another cry. Followed by the sound of something, or someone, falling.

Quietly the Executioner twisted the knob. Locked. He sprinted to the corner, counting four shop fronts as he passed. Turning the corner, he ducked into the alley that ran behind the buildings.

Hurdling overturned trash receptacles and scattered litter, the warrior backtracked through the alley to the fourth building. The back door, like the front, was locked.

The Executioner took a split second to evaluate the situation. The splintery wood door would yield under his foot, but the inevitable noise would warn the occupants of the shop of his presence. Stepping back from the faded yellow brick, he took a better look at the building.

A lone window, open, was visible on the second floor. He dragged a trash can from the other side of the alley and set it under the window, climbed atop and leaped upward, grasping the sill with both hands. Rotten wood creaked, threatening to give way under his weight as he pulled himself up, all the while wondering if someone would blow his head off when it cleared the top. Instead, he peered into an empty room littered with discarded scraps of Sheetrock and wood.

Bolan pulled himself through the opening and dropped lightly to the floor. Below, he heard the muffled voices once more, then a slapping sound. He crept to the door and eased it open.

Winding, rickety wooden stairs led downward. The voices were clearer now, and the fact that the Executioner couldn't translate the words made little difference in discerning their tone.

Two men screamed and threatened as a third periodically tried to break into the "conversation." Each interruption was followed by a slap. The third voice spoke in the rapid semiwhine of a man attempting to talk himself out of trouble.

No, fluency in the Turkish language wasn't necessary to pick up on what was happening below. In fact, it would have been no help at all.

The voices below spoke the language of Iran. Farsi.

Bolan looked at the stairs. There was no way to descend without giving himself away. At best his first step would send the squeaking sound of ancient wood echoing downstairs. At worst the steps would give way and he'd plummet to the floor below.

There remained only one course of action. He'd have to descend the stairs as quickly as possible, hoping to overtake the men below before they reacted to the sudden noise.

And hope the wood didn't disintegrate beneath his weight.

The warrior retraced his steps to the room behind him, digging quietly through the rubble until he found a three-foot scrap of two-by-four. He wondered briefly what weapons the men below might carry. Knives or swords, if he was lucky. Guns, if he wasn't. Had his luck run out?

He returned to the stairs just in time to hear the muffled voices whisper as the front door closed. The dictates of the battle suddenly altered, Bolan crept cautiously down the steps, the wooden bludgeon gripped before him in both hands.

The musty smell of long-stored rugs grew stronger as he descended the winding steps. Reaching the ground floor, he found himself in a storage room that was packed floor to ceiling with carpets. Crouched and ready, his eyes swept the room in a quick 180.

Nothing. Bolan saw light creeping from under the closed door. The same light he'd seen from the street? It had to be. The building's dimensions wouldn't permit more than one more small area between where he stood and the front showroom. Moving to the door, the Executioner dropped to his knees and peered through the keyhole.

The smell of fresh paint assaulted him. Freshly taped Sheetrock covered the walls and contrasted sharply with the old-world effect of the intricate handwoven carpet on the floor.

A massive oak desk faced the opposite wall. Behind it, back to Bolan, sat a man in a caftan and keffiyeh.

The warrior didn't need to look further to know what had happened. Far stronger than the smell of the paint, the fetid, familiar odor of death rose to the Executioner's nostrils.

He threw open the door and walked to the desk. Hossein's throat gaped from ear to ear in a gruesome parody of a smile. The muscles of the dead man's neck still pulsed reflexively as blood gushed onto his chest.

The Executioner had found the right Hossein.

Sometimes you *did* get lucky. Sometimes you just thought you had.

3

Mehmed Hasan Darazi watched the major's body swing slowly in the breeze that circulated through the cave. He had thanked Allah for that breeze—a gift from paradise. Without it the humid heat the sun brought to the stone walls each day would have been unbearable.

The hostages were quieting as the hoods were replaced over their heads. Their reactions to the first of the executions had been a mixture of awe and agony, sniffles and screams. One man, an American banker, had defecated in his pants, and the Hizbullah leader had been forced to send outside for fresh pajamas. Had it been only the hostage's discomfort at stake, Darazi would have left him in his soiled garments. But the stench within the cave would soon have become unbearable to the soldiers of jihad—the holy war against the infidels.

The banker looked ridiculous now, sitting hooded, naked from the waist down, his hands attempting to cover genitals shriveled from fear. Darazi smiled. He'd taken pleasure in beating the American, and he could still hear the quiet sobbing his blows had produced.

Turning toward the video camera in front of the scaffold, the Hizbullah leader heard the quiet purr as the tape rewound, then watched as Khalid pulled it from the camera and replaced it within the plastic cover.

Television. Videos. Inventions of the Western infidels. But they would serve his purpose.

"Harun!" Darazi shouted suddenly and waited as a short, emaciated man scurried forward.

"Yes, Mehmed?" he asked.

The leader took the tape from Khalid and handed it to the man. "You are to see that this is safely transported to the news media. Employ someone through whom you cannot be traced."

"The country is full of those starving at the hands of the infidels," Harun said. "In the name of Allah and his earthly representative, Mehmed, I will secure the aid of—"

Darazi waved a hand in front of his face. "Go."

The Hizbullah messenger bent forward slightly, then hurried to one of the small boats tied at the edge of the cave's rock floor. He started the motor and disappeared into the dimly lit waterway leading out of the cave.

A few hours without the sycophant would be relaxing. His bootlicking had grown tiresome to the Hizbullah leader, and it was becoming a full-time job to keep the devious little man's hands off the blond woman.

He glanced quickly at the American woman, her face hidden beneath the black hood. He felt an involuntary tightness in his groin as he stared at the breasts that strained against the thin gray material of the pajamas.

Darazi walked silently across the stone to where
Sharon Walker sat. It pleased him that she didn't
know he had approached. Standing next to her, he
could see the slight shiver as her shoulders periodically spasmed. He knelt silently, leaning forward to
bring his face within inches of her own and reveling in
the power of invisibility the hood gave him. He
breathed deeply, silently, luxuriating in her scent. Her
essence was in many ways like the Mideastern women
he had known—yet somehow so different.

He stood and walked away. No. She had defiled
herself. She was unclean.

Turning his attention back to the swinging body, the
Shiite felt his lust turn to hatred. "Cut him down," he
snarled to two of the men. "He is to be wrapped and
taken away. Frozen. One never knows what turn
events may take. We may have further use for the
body."

He paused, thinking briefly of the Iranian airliner
shot from the skies by the Americans. The fools had
suspected that the bodies on board had already been
dead before the plane left the ground, but they'd never
successfully proved those suspicions to the rest of the
world.

Hearing the sounds of boats in the tunnel, he moved
to the edge of the rock. Ali and Dawud had returned.

Ali stepped from the boat and approached. "The
other hostages have been secured," the tall man announced.

Darazi nodded and watched silently as Ali returned
to the boat and helped Dawud unload food and other
provisions, carrying the large boxes across the rock
and piling them against the wall behind the scaffold.

Darazi stared at the muscles in Ali's forearms as the big man hefted a massive box of rice. Though his junior by almost a decade, Ali's large build and general appearance made the leader think of his father.

Abdul Darazi hadn't been Iranian, but Turkish, and it was from that heritage that both Mehmed and his brother had received their names. A roving frontier champion of the holy war, Mehmed's father had been a Sunni Muslim. Alone and without money in his wanderings through Iran, he'd been befriended by a group of Kurds who had settled in Esfahan. Abdul had fallen in love and married one of the women, who gave birth to twin sons.

Abdul had become a Shiite, converting to Allah's true will after meeting and marrying Mehmed's mother. But the spirit of adventure had been Allah's gift to Abdul. The converted Sunni had been a fighter, and the lust for action still coursed throughout his veins. Mehmed's earliest memories were of his father's periodic absences. Then, on the morning of the twins' fifth birthday, Mehmed had risen to find his mother weeping and his father and brother gone.

His mother's words returned to him now, as clearly as if she were there with him in the cave.

"He's a soldier, Mehmed. He has returned to the fight. This time to do battle on the side of Allah."

As had happened on his fifth birthday, an odd union of pride and sorrow crept over Mehmed Darazi—pride that he was the son of such a brave and dedicated warrior. Sorrow that he had never again seen either his father or brother.

Again, as so many times throughout his life, he wondered briefly why his father had chosen his brother rather than himself as the one to accompany him, to be trained in the ways of a warrior. And once again, as he always did, he pushed the uncomfortable thought from his mind.

Allah had His reasons and His plan. He would reveal all in time.

The Hizbullah leader took a last look at the American woman as he crossed the cave toward the small dugout hidden from view in the rocks. He entered the cavern and collapsed into an armchair next to the table that held a small brass oil lamp. Lighting the wick of the lamp, he leaned back and felt the chair's cool leather upholstery against his arms.

The leather armchair had been manufactured in America. It was another example of the past—of a time when the warriors of Allah had been subjugated to the economic power of the West.

It wasn't a proper throne for a man named after Mehmed the Conqueror, the great-grandfather of Süleyman, and the man who had taken Constantinople back from the heretics and built it into Istanbul. Mehmed the Conqueror had been a mighty Turkish warrior-sheikh in an era when world power rested where it belonged—within the Kingdom of Allah.

He closed his eyes, feeling his fingers encircle the armrests and dig into the leather like talons. Jihad was approaching. The power of the world would soon return to its rightful heirs. Allah would once again rule the earth. And Mehmed Darazi would be His representative. He would be king.

WITH HOSSEIN'S MURDER, the Executioner's only possible lead to the hostages had drained away as swiftly as the blood flowing from the carpet dealer's throat.

Bolan pressed his foot down on the accelerator, forcing the sluggish Fiat down the highway toward the frontier outpost of Yayladag on the Syrian border. He glanced at his watch.

The time bomb was ticking. Four and a half days remained before Sharon Walker would be hanged from the same scaffold from which Bolan had watched Randolph Groethe sway.

And who knew what hell the terrorists might put the woman through before killing her? So far the captors had gone out of their way to show that none of the women had been molested. In their quest to intimidate the Western powers and Israel, they had wisely chosen not to let sex get in the way of their objectives. The Hizbullah leaders knew instinctively that once they stooped to rape, many of their sympathizers would be upset.

But what about a woman who was close to execution?

Bolan had seen Sharon Walker on the video. In spite of her terrified eyes and the tears rolling down her cheeks, he'd seen what the Hizbullah men would have gazed upon daily throughout her two-year captivity—a beautiful and desirable woman.

Confined within the constraints that the terrorists' mission required, there'd be little chance for sexual release. As the days grew to months and the months became years, their minds would cloud, their objectives become less clear, as they were deprived of biological satisfaction. Actions that might have seemed preposterous at first would appear more rational. And with Sharon Walker at the brink of death, anyway, they might see no reason that their desire shouldn't be fulfilled.

Like dead men, dead women told no tales.

Bolan chased the train of thought from his mind; it would do no good to dwell on what might happen. Far better to concentrate on developing a plan of attack that would ensure that it didn't.

Pulling the Fiat to a halt on the road's gravel shoulder, he threw the gearshift into neutral. What was his next move? He had only one option—a long shot.

He'd drive on to Syria, then Lebanon, to the streets of Beirut where the eye of the storm was raging. If a clue could be found, he would find it there. The Executioner threw the car into gear and continued through the barren hills toward Yayladag and the Syrian border.

There were three approaches he could take in crossing the border, and each one had its drawbacks. There was no doubt in Bolan's mind that by this time the customs men in Ankara had learned that Mike McKay had never checked into the Buyuk.

So what did that mean? To what extent would they go to find him? The Executioner couldn't help believing that had the authorities really suspected his involvement with the terrorists on the plane, he'd never have been allowed to leave the airport in the first place.

But if he tried to cross into Syria under the McKay identity, and the border guards *had* been alerted, the game would come to a screeching halt.

His second alternative was just as risky. Pat Harding's passport still had no entry stamp. Bolan could do his best to bluff it through—customs agents were people, and people made mistakes. It wouldn't be the first time a busy or disinterested civil servant had forgotten to verify a foreigner's entry into the country.

But at the very least he'd be turned back to obtain proper documentation before being allowed to depart Turkey. This would expend too much time, which was a precious commodity at the moment.

The third option consisted of ditching the Fiat somewhere near the border and crossing, unseen, on foot. Bolan had no doubt he could pull it off, but he hesitated to employ this tactic. He'd have to cross twenty miles of semidesert scrub country before he reached the nearest town.

That, in itself, presented no problem for the soldier. But his fast itinerary made no provisions for nature treks.

As he rounded a hilly curve and saw the Turkish guardhouse ahead, the Executioner realized he had only one logical course of action.

Mike McKay had done all right so far. He'd paid his money and taken his chances, and so far he'd blackjacked every hand. It was time for McKay to take one more card from the dealer.

Paint peeled from the shabby white wood of the guardhouse. A quarter mile in the distance he saw a similar structure on the Syrian side of the border. Bolan watched a uniformed guard step down from the building as he slowed. The man smiled pleasantly, raising the clipboard in his hand and guiding the Fiat to a halt. Bolan rolled down the window and extended his passport.

"Mehaba," the guard said.

Bolan smiled, shrugging.

"American?"

Bolan nodded.

The guard nodded back, glancing from the warrior's passport picture to his face, the smile still beaming.

While the guard studied the document, Bolan glanced down the road to the Syrian point of entry. Two uniformed men, one leaning on the handle of a small lawn mower, chatted outside the building.

"You are taking any antique from Turkey, Mr. McKay?" the guard asked.

Bolan turned back to him and smiled, shaking his head. "Wish I could afford them."

The guard nodded. "Carpets?"

"Same problem."

"Narcotics?"

"No."

"You have any weapon or ammunitions, Mr. McKay?" the guard asked.

"No."

The guard stepped into the tiny building. Bolan watched through the door as he grabbed a rubber stamp from the table next to the shortwave radio. He brought the stamp down with a loud thud, then returned to the Fiat and handed the passport back through the window.

"Visit Turkey agai—" The guard was interrupted by a sudden burst over the shortwave. "One moment," he said, stepping back into the shack.

Bolan watched as the man listened attentively to the excited voice over the radio. Then, slowly, the guard's eyes turned toward the Executioner. His smile faded.

The scratchy radio voice raved on as the man's hand moved casually toward the flap on his holster.

Had he spoken fluent Turkish the Executioner couldn't have understood the radio message more clearly. Glancing quickly down the road to the Syrian checkpoint, he saw the guards still standing around the lawn mower.

Bolan floored the Fiat's accelerator. The tiny engine sputtered, then caught, jerking him back against the seat just as the Turkish guard's gun cleared leather.

The warrior was halfway to the Syrian guard shack and slamming the Fiat's screaming engine into fourth gear before the two men realized what was happening. One man let go of the mower handle and fumbled for the gun at his side, which fell from his holster into the grass. His compatriot wasn't as clumsy. Taking a step back from the roadway, he drew his revolver and waited as the Fiat neared.

Bolan watched him aim as his target came into range. The Executioner ground the gearshift down to third as the man fired, the Fiat jerking and whining as the bullet ricocheted harmlessly off the pavement three feet in front of the bumper. Gunning the engine, the warrior returned the car to fourth and sailed past into Syria.

In the rearview mirror he saw a Turkish jeep racing down the road to the Syrian station. Bolan reached over his shoulder and secured the seat belt and shoulder harness around him. The chase had only begun.

4

Bolan kept his foot to the floor, urging the lazy engine down the highway. There was no way the Fiat could outrun the troops who would soon mount the hunt.

But the Executioner had one advantage. The Syrian border guards had been totally unprepared for action, and he hoped that in the time it took them to organize he could lose himself somewhere within the country.

He had a chance, but the chance was thin.

Bolan scanned the roadway ahead as he drove. The outpost guards' first action would be to radio for assistance. If there happened to be Syrian troops in the immediate area, they'd whittle his chance from thin to anorexic.

Holding the wheel steady with his left hand, he leaned across the seat and pulled a road map from the glove compartment. The nearest town of any size was Al-Haffah, a short jaunt off the road to Latakia. The small village of Jisr ash-Shughur lay closer, slightly to the east, and unless he missed his guess he should be approaching the junction soon.

Bolan dropped the map onto the passenger seat as the Fiat glided past a deserted sheep trail. He considered the path briefly, then rejected it as another time-consuming option.

Latakia was out of the question. At least fifty miles. Regardless of how incompetent they might have appeared at the border, the Syrian forces would have plenty of time to close off the highways before he reached the coastal city. Al-Haffah might be slightly closer, but it looked to be little larger than Jisr ash-Shughur on the map. He'd be readily noticed in either place.

It was six of one, half a dozen of the other. But he had to make a decision—fast.

Bolan topped a ridge. The intersection was three hundred feet ahead. He tapped the brakes lightly, slowing for the turn just as two Syrian troop transport vehicles crested the hill on the other side of the junction and raced to meet him from the opposite direction.

The Executioner stomped hard on the brake pedal. Tires shrieking, the Fiat slid along the highway toward the carriers. Sand and pebbles flew around the car in a miniature tornado as Bolan twirled the steering wheel, reversing direction.

The sheep trail was no longer an inconvenient option. There was no other choice.

Bolan had no doubt that pursuit from the Turkish border would be nearing, hoping to sandwich him between the troops that bore down from the south. If he could outdistance the heavy transport vehicles at his rear, and reach the trail before being cut off by the oncoming company, he still stood a chance.

Gears grinding as he worked the shift, Bolan maneuvered the Fiat back along the road through the foothills. He glanced periodically in the rearview mirror. The massive troop vehicles weren't gaining any ground.

They weren't losing any, either.

He rounded a curve and came face-to-face with three more Syrian troop carriers. Rifles extended from the open truck beds as the soldiers in the point vehicle opened fire.

Bolan inspected the roadway ahead. He would confront the lead truck as both parties entered the narrow slopes between two foothills flanking the highway.

Two rounds struck the windshield, and glass shattered over the warrior as he raised a forearm to protect his eyes.

There was no time to stop. He grasped the wheel tightly in both hands as the trucks neared in a deadly game of chicken. At the last instant he swerved from the road, across the thin shoulder and up the side of the foothill. The Fiat's right side rose to a forty-five-degree angle as the tires climbed the embankment.

More rounds skimmed off the hood as Bolan came abreast of the convoy, the Fiat threatening to flip over. Sparks flew to his left as the hubcaps scraped the pavement before dislodging and bounding away behind him.

Bolan returned to the highway, bringing the Fiat back into control as soon as he'd passed the last vehicle. In the mirror he saw several of the troops leap from the rear truck as the convoy slowed to reverse direction. One of the soldiers knelt, raised his rifle and sighted down the barrel.

Bolan pushed harder on the gas. Leaning forward, he tried to will potency into the Fiat's tiny engine. Then he heard the sharp crack of the rifle, followed by another explosion as his left rear tire blew behind him. The warrior fought the wheel, trying to turn into the skid as the Fiat fishtailed down the road toward a bridge. He tapped the brake lightly as the car neared the dry ravine below the railing.

The bridge loomed large as the Executioner finally stood on the brake in a final, desperate act to slow the vehicle. He felt the Fiat lurch left toward the center of the road, then spin wildly as the car slammed through the bridge railing and over the edge.

The warrior grasped the shoulder harness as the Fiat rolled end over end down the side of the ravine. It finally came to a stop at the bottom of the incline, upside down.

Bolan shook the cobwebs from his head, fighting the urge to vomit. Still dizzy, he dragged himself through the window and leaned against the overturned vehicle.

Above, on the highway, he could hear the whine of the truck engines as they raced to the bridge. He scanned his surroundings. Hills and valleys, but nothing that offered long-term concealment. And he was in no condition at the moment for a footrace across the Syrian plains. What he needed was a diversion. Fast.

Bolan smelled the gas before he saw it and looked down at the car. Sometime during the onslaught a round had torn through the tank, and gas now dripped onto the sandy ground, forming a rapidly widening pool at his feet.

Kneeling, the Executioner squeezed back through the driver's window and rolled onto his back. Locating the ashtray, he tore open the drawer and depressed the cigarette lighter.

Above him on the road he heard the transport vehicles slowing as they approached the ravine. The seconds ticked away—an eternity—as he waited for the lighter to heat. Suddenly the round metal tube popped outward, and the Executioner ripped it from its housing.

Worming back through the window, he stood and sprinted under the bridge. Then, turning, he lobbed the lighter through the air toward the puddle of gas by the tank.

For a brief moment he thought he'd missed, then flames blossomed next to the Fiat, and a second later the car burst into a fiery inferno, driving the Executioner farther under the bridge just as the first head appeared on the ridge.

Excited voices heralded the arrival of more soldiers, who crowded to the edge of the ravine, pushing and shoving to see. Clawing dirt with both hands, the warrior climbed up under the bridge, twisting sideways at the top and pressing his body into the crevice where steel met earth.

The Executioner closed his eyes, taking advantage of the brief reprieve to evaluate the situation. Listening, he heard a brusque voice, obviously in command. Bolan knew a search of the immediate area would be ordered.

Still hidden by the steel and concrete over his head, he crawled back down the embankment. He paused briefly at the bottom, risking a quick glance around the girders supporting the bridge.

One soldier began to descend the steep slope toward the smoke and flames. He stopped halfway down, his forearm shielding his face against the heat, then returned to the top, shaking his head.

It would be some time yet before the fire died down and it was determined for certain that he wasn't in the car. Until then any search they mounted would be halfhearted at best. But they would stay close to the Fiat, concentrating on the immediate area.

The Executioner moved to the other side of the bridge. Dropping prone, he felt the sting of sand and dirt in the cuts on his face and arms. Blood gushed from a gash over his eyebrow, dripping onto the ground. He pulled the shirt over his head, wrapping the wound, then covered the red splashes with sand.

There was no sense in leaving a trail of bread crumbs.

Painfully he pulled himself forward, belly-crawling from under the bridge and into the thorny brush on the opposite side of the burning Fiat. He had no idea where the dry ravine led, but it didn't matter, just as long as it got him out of the vicinity.

Behind and above, the Executioner heard more orders, then the sound of footsteps as the men spread out. He continued down the winding ravine, trying to maintain a delicate balance of speed and silence. Some of the men had descended the slope on his side of the bridge, and he heard swishing sounds as their rifles poked and probed the undergrowth.

From the ridge above came the footsteps of a lone searcher following the ravine. As the steps neared, the

Executioner froze, hugging the gritty earth beneath his chest.

The footsteps passed.

Bolan risked a quick look, raising his head from the prickly scrub. The soldier was in front of him now, both rifle and eyes scanning the gully below.

Blood oozed through the soaked shirt-bandage as Bolan dragged himself farther with wrists and elbows, pausing periodically to hide the drops in the sand. He rounded a bend in the ravine and could hear the noise made by the soldier as the man doubled back.

The Executioner twisted, glancing behind. He'd covered only a hundred yards since crawling from under the bridge. In the distance he saw the tiny figures of the Syrians as they continued probing the underbrush.

The soldier in front drew nearer, closing in on a direct path to the Executioner. Bolan figured he had a minute, max, before the rifle barrel poked downward to discover him.

He rolled quietly to his left into a thicket of scrub at the edge of the gully. Turning onto his back, he dug silently at the soft earth at his sides, dropping handfuls of sand and dirt onto his chest and pants. He had no time to dig himself out of sight, but if he could create enough camouflage to break his general outline, there was still a possibility that the soldier might overlook him.

Bolan scooped a double handful of sand into his hair just as the Syrian's legs appeared through the thicket. Three feet from where the Executioner lay, the man paused, glanced quickly around, then muttered something under his breath.

The warrior lay stock-still as the man unbuttoned the flap of his shirt pocket and produced a package of cigarettes. He removed one from the pack, lighted it and inhaled deeply.

Suddenly he turned and strode purposefully toward the thicket, his brown combat boot halting an inch from the Executioner's leg. Through the thorns and barbs of the brush, Bolan saw the soldier frown as he scanned the ground next to the thicket. Finally the man stomped the earth in several places, shrugged and turned away.

Bolan waited until the soldier's footsteps died in the distance before rolling out of the thicket. Staying prone, he continued through the winding ravine as it gradually rose to meet the ground. When the depression finally became too shallow to afford cover, Bolan turned back.

The bridge, and the Syrian troops, were no longer in sight.

Rising to his feet, he felt a wave of exhaustion start in his head. It flowed through his chest, down his legs and into his feet. The head wound had stopped bleeding, but Bolan suspected his sudden fatigue was a result of blood loss.

Forcing his aching legs to move over the scrubland, Bolan eventually covered what he guessed was ten miles. Finally, when weariness threatened to drop him in his tracks, he spotted the town in the distance.

Jisr ash-Shughur. The hard way.

He stopped to rest under the limbs of a scraggly tree, dropping to the sand. He felt the muscles in his face contract as he tried to concentrate, doing his best to force the haziness and fatigue from his mind.

The Syrian troops would continue their half-serious search until the flames died down. Then, finding no remains of a body in the Fiat, the area to be scrutinized would be widened.

And the search would begin in earnest.

He had to make it to Jisr ash-Shughur, had to find a place to hole up until his strength returned.

Bolan glanced across the horizon at the tiny village in the distance. The buildings seemed to wave and shimmer under the fiery desert sun.

Pay someone . . . he could pay someone to put him up.

In the distance the buildings began to diminish.

People were...poor...needed money...pay someone to . . . hide . . . him.

The warrior's knees buckled and he fell to the sand.

When he awoke, Bolan had no idea how long he'd slept. Although still slightly dizzy, he was conscious of two things—he hadn't lost as much blood as he'd feared, as most of his strength had returned, and he was surrounded by twenty men on horses and camels, all dressed as if they'd just stepped out of *One Thousand and One Arabian Nights*.

SHARON WALKER SQUINTED when the hood was removed. Across the cave she saw one of the terrorists ladling rice into bowls. Rice, rice and more rice. Sharon had decided months ago that if she ever returned to America, rice would never again pass her lips.

Her eyes moved to the far wall of the cave past the scaffold. Behind it, next to the tall stack of boxes, the four members of Group One slept in bunk beds. Sharon had been assigned to Group Two, which had consisted of four hostages as well until . . .

She forced the image of Rand Groethe, neck broken at the end of the rope, from her mind. She couldn't afford to think about him right now.

As she watched, the guard began waking the sleeping forms in the beds. She pulled her knees tightly under her chin and wrapped her arms around her calves. It was time for Group One's baths. She turned her eyes away as the hostages, still groggy from sleep, rose from the bunk beds and walked to the edge of the rock floor. One of the women began disrobing behind a sheet held by a guard.

Sharon glanced toward the wall nearest her. A short, seedy-looking man stood leaning against the rock, his eyes glued to the water where the nude woman now bathed. The man's right hand cupped his groin and Sharon could see the tendons in his forearm contract every few seconds when he squeezed. Catching her stare, he jerked his hand away, his eyes moving just as quickly.

The other terrorists called the man Harun. Sharon Walker called him "Hands." Once, she'd made the mistake of calling him that to his face and had received several violent slaps. Was that why she'd been chosen as the next to die?

No, it wasn't. Sharon Walker knew all too well what had decreed the death sentence for Rand Groethe and herself.

She saw Harun out of the corner of her eye as he approached. "Groupa Do," he shouted.

Groupa Do. Group Two. It was time for her bath.

Sharon rose and followed the others to the edge of the water. Stepping behind the sheet Harun extended, she unbuttoned the pajama top and dropped it to the floor. She saw the man's shifty eyes on her body as they peered over the sheet, felt them as clearly as his hands when the hood was in place. Tossing the bottoms of her pajamas onto the rock, she lowered herself as casually as possible over the edge.

She wondered briefly why modesty had never left her during the long months of captivity. Some of the others, even those who'd been humiliated at first, now seemed as comfortable as children in their nudity.

Taking the soap from the ledge, she began lathering her arms. Then she glanced up quickly. Harun's gaze was glued to her breasts, half-visible under the water. The terrorist's lips twisted into a foolish grin, and his hand had returned to his crotch. This time he made no effort to move it when their eyes met.

Turning her back to the man, Sharon looked down the tunnel that led outside—to freedom. She wondered briefly what her chances of swimming might be. A sardonic smile distorted her face.

She'd planned escape, at first. They all had—Rand Groethe most of all. But as the hopelessness of their situation became clear, the will to escape had disappeared.

Where would she go if she did make it out of the cave? Who would help her? Who could she trust to guide her to safety rather than return her to these pious, distorted murderers masquerading as holy men?

None of the Americans had talked about escape for over a year. No one except Rand Groethe.

Sharon rinsed her hair and reached for the towel Harun extended. Wrapping it around her body, she pulled herself up onto the ledge and stepped back behind the sheet. As she dropped the towel, she saw Harun's face leer over the sheet. Then, from behind him, she heard the sharp, biting voice of the leader, and Harun turned away.

She finished dressing and joined the rest of Group Two as they followed Harun back across the massive cavern to their seats on the floor. Sharon sat down, thinking of Rand Groethe.

She saw Harun in front of her, a hood in his hands. A deep, empty feeling of hopelessness swept through her as the grinning man slid the dark sack over her head.

5

The Executioner rose to his feet and watched as a mounted man in a black-and-white-striped keffiyeh slid his rifle into a scabbard, swung both legs over his horse's neck and dropped to the ground. The ebony horn handle of a long Khyber fighting knife extended over the top of the tattered sash that cinched his tunic at the waist. The tips of the man's flowing mustache curled upward, oiled with some form of lubricant.

As he scanned the rest of the party, Bolan wondered briefly who they were. Nomads of some type. An odd assortment of contemporary and antiquated weaponry poked out of their sashes. He spotted a Prelaz Burnard percussion rifle in the hands of a man who also carried a new hollow-handled BuckMaster survival knife. Scattered throughout the group were rusting Webley revolvers and ball-and-cap pistols, as well as a Detonics Pocket 9 and an AK-47. On the hip of one man, extending through a cutout snub-nosed holster, Bolan saw the stainless-steel barrel of a Smith and Wesson Model 66.

The band's shabby clothing reflected its poverty, but some of the weapons disputed it. The seeming contradiction left only one explanation—whoever the men were, they were thieves.

Bolan studied the mustachioed man as he neared. An expensive SwissChamp multitool knife dangled from a lanyard next to the Khyber, and it hadn't come from the neighborhood sporting goods store. Neither had the Model 66 or the BuckMaster.

The man with the flowing mustache came to a halt three feet in front of Bolan. He scrutinized the Executioner, then screamed into his face in an unrecognizable language. Bolan returned the stare.

The shouting continued, and although the words were mostly unintelligible, Bolan could tell that the man had switched to an Arabic dialect. Getting no response again, the angry man's hand moved to the hilt of the Khyber knife.

Bolan took a half step in and grabbed the man's arm before the blade could clear his sash. He twisted in and down, trapping the hand against the rough cloth, the wrist bent at a painful angle. The nomad screamed and dropped to his knees, his face grimacing in agony.

The swish of cloth, followed by the clicking sounds of many weapons cocking, reached Bolan's ears. Slowly he released the wrist and stepped back.

The man on the ground got to his feet, his eyes blazing embers of hatred. Sprinting back to his horse, he remounted and yanked his rifle from the scabbard. Bolan held his ground, waiting. The rifle barrel pointed at the warrior, then swung sideways as the bandit leader motioned him forward across the sand.

As they topped a sandy ridge ten minutes later, Bolan spotted the camp. Bony sheep and goats grazed lethargically on sparse grass near the tents while unveiled women lugged earthen water jugs back and forth from the camp to the small oasis.

An ancient Studebaker pickup stood near the center of camp. Next to it was an aged flatbed loaded with barrels. Bolan saw two dozen small tents surrounding a massive dwelling that looked to be woven of camel hair and wool. A ten-foot statue of a peacock, wings outstretched, sat next to the tent's closed flap.

As they neared, the tent flap opened and a bare-chested man of amazing proportions stepped outside. Standing erect, his head barely reached the midway point of the peacock, but Bolan guessed his weight to be near three hundred pounds. The shiny silk of his headdress gleamed in the sunlight as he scratched the rolls of fat and hair at his abdomen.

The man snapped his fingers, and a soft feminine arm extended through the opening, holding an immense robe. The fat man threw the garment over his shoulders and waddled forward to meet them.

Eyes moving past the Executioner, the fat man thundered orders to the nomads. Bolan heard the men dismount and wondered again who these people might be. There was something odd, something indefinable, that set them apart from the other Mideast nomads he'd known.

Kurds? That seemed more likely. Their language sounded as if it could be a dialect of Kirmanji.

The fat man snapped his fingers and a woman rushed to him. At a short, harsh order the woman bowed, then turned and trotted away.

A moment later Bolan saw the flap of a smaller tent open and a tall, broad-chested man stepped forth. He swaggered confidently forward, taking a position next to his chief. Bolan was surprised to see that he stood well over six feet, a rarity for men of the desert.

Heredity and poor nutrition usually combined to ensure that the nomads remained far below average height.

There was something vaguely familiar about the tall man's face. Bolan searched his memory, but came up empty.

The man wore a camel hair tunic and loose-fitting pantaloons. He listened briefly to the chief, then turned to the Executioner. "American, I assume?" he said in British-accented English.

Bolan tried to hide his surprise. He nodded.

"Ah, then I will interpret." He turned back to the chief as the fat man mumbled something.

"Sheikh Zarbani wishes to know if you have obtained a permit to cross his land."

Bolan shrugged. There was no point in playing the game. He could guess what was coming.

"If no permit has been obtained, it must be purchased now." The tall man grinned. "It's a tax of sorts. Or think of it as one of your American turnpikes."

Bolan stared the man in the eye. The Executioner had money. He *could* obtain a "permit." If the situation was slightly different, that would be the wisest thing to do. And he had no doubt that these bandits would accept the Turkish liras in his pocket.

They'd accept it all right. All of it.

If he lost his finances here, he'd have nothing to operate on as he moved toward Sharon Walker and the other hostages.

"Sorry," Bolan said bluntly. "No money."

The interpreter looked him up and down again, pausing briefly to inspect the gash over his brow.

"Yes. It appears your trip hasn't been pleasant. Perhaps you have already met with some of our brothers?" He paused again, laughing at his joke. "What have you to trade?"

"Nothing."

The interpreter reported to the chief. The fat man nodded and barked something in reply.

The tall man turned back to Bolan and shrugged indifferently. "Then you will die."

Walking swiftly to the chief's tent, the man entered and reappeared a moment later with a long wooden box. Setting the box in the sand at Bolan's feet, he knelt and flipped the brass clasps on the side. "My people have an ancient custom. The tradition is steeped in history and tradition—but I won't bore you with the details. You wouldn't understand."

"Try me," Bolan replied. "I might surprise you."

The Syrian shook his head as he opened the lid. "It doesn't matter. You won't live long enough to contemplate the significance if you *do* understand."

Drawing a pair of matched Choora knives from the box, the man stood. "You must fight our foremost warrior, and you need only know that to emerge victorious is to live." A slight chuckle shook the man's chest. "To be defeated...is to die." He extended both knives, hilt first, to the Executioner.

Bolan glanced down at the nickel-silver medallions set in smooth buffalo horn handles. Arab geometrical decorations ran the length of the steel, from guard to tip, on both sides of the T-rib that reinforced the blade back.

The Executioner reached out and grasped the hilt of one of the knives. He scanned the crowd of men seated in the sand, then returned his gaze to the man who stood in front of him.

Bolan knew the answer to the question before he asked. "And just who *is* your foremost warrior?"

The tall man smiled and bowed slightly. Flipping the remaining Choora into the air, he caught it in a saber grip as it fell.

"Any rules to this game?" Bolan asked.

The nomad began to circle, the knife clutched in his right hand. "Only one." His face twisted into a smile. "Stay alive as long as you can."

Bolan nodded. He moved slowly, matching his adversary's steps, trying to get a handle on the fighting style he faced. The Executioner had no idea what to expect. The Choora's twelve-inch blade meant that the weapon fell somewhere between knife and sword, and a combination of techniques from both disciplines might be used.

Around him Bolan heard the quiet voices of the spectators. From the corner of his eye he saw coins and crumpled bills being pressed into the hand of a laughing man with sores covering his face.

The tall nomad reversed directions and began to circle toward Bolan's right. The Executioner adjusted accordingly, mirroring the man's movements.

Suddenly the nomad's knife flashed forward like a spear. Bolan took a half step to his left, twisted at the waist and let the blade pass a mere inch from his ribs. Whirling his torso back toward the man, he delivered a slashing cut across the back of his adversary's hand.

Blood gushed from the open wound. Shock replaced the grin, then his eyes narrowed and he resumed circling.

Again the nomad lunged, this time dropping low. His knife sliced a wicked arc toward Bolan's thigh as his other arm shot backward to maintain balance in the low, wide-legged stance.

Bolan jumped back as the blade whistled by, then stepped in, aiming a snap kick toward the nomad's head. He was a split second slow. The desert fighter fell to his knees, rolled sideways and sprang back to his feet, brandishing his knife in a lightning series of X-slashes aimed at the Executioner's face.

Bolan retreated, dodging, then stepped forward as his enemy leaped in with a vicious overhead stroke. The Executioner's forearm slid under the razor-honed blade, blocking the nomad's wrist. Bolan took another sliding step and tried to knee the guy in the groin, but the nomad twisted away, the blow striking his knee.

But the Executioner's attack hadn't been wasted. Limping now, the desert warrior's circles grew smaller, his footwork slowing as he winced in pain. He grimaced and pulled his last ace from his sleeve.

Dropping suddenly to the ground, he landed on his side and hooked both legs around the Executioner's feet. Bolan glanced down as the guy's legs clamped together in an attempt to take him to the sand.

There was nowhere to go but up.

The Executioner sprang with his calves, pulling his heels up behind him as the desert fighter's legs struck together below. He landed on the balls of his feet, shuffled to the side and brought his foot down in a vicious stomp to the ribs.

The nomad grunted in pain as Bolan dropped his knees onto the man's chest, caught the guy's bloody wrist and pinned the weapon to the ground. The Executioner twirled his knife overhead and saw the instinctive fear in the nomad's eyes as the man's body fell slack in preparation for death.

Slowly Bolan rose to his feet. The man's dark eyes opened wide. "What? You won't kill me?"

Bolan shook his head. "No point in it." He dropped his knife into the sand.

The man on the ground rose unsteadily, walked slowly to the Executioner, then prostrated himself. "My life is yours," he said simply.

Bolan reached down and hauled the man to his feet. "Your life's your own," he growled. He glanced quickly at the men seated around them, listening to the excited talk as money changed hands. The man with the sores on his face now wore a mournful expression as he redistributed the money among the others.

The Executioner turned back to the nomad. "I don't want your life, but I could use some help."

A CRUDE HEDGE of brushwood had been built outside the sheikh's tent to form a small courtyard. A fire blazed in the center of the enclosure.

Mack Bolan sat astride a camel saddle in the courtyard between the sheikh and Muhibbi—the man whose life the Executioner had spared. Several tribesmen had joined them, forming a crescent in the sand at the feet of the trio.

A ginger-skinned woman who looked to be in her mid-twenties approached, carrying an earthen water jug. Gold and silver amulets, in the shape of human hands, hung from her neck. Half hidden in the long tresses of ink-black hair, Bolan saw a matching set of golden hands dangling from her ears.

But it was her pale blue eyes that riveted his attention. Contrasting starkly with her dark skin and hair, they reminded Bolan of the Aryan origins of many of the peoples in the Mideast. Bowing slightly to the sheikh, she turned to Bolan and repeated the motion, then handed him the water jug. The faded azure eyes met his for a moment, then fell to the ground in embarrassment.

Bolan watched as the tribeswomen finished their preparations for the evening meal. Talking excitedly, they eventually disappeared into the tent until only the matron who'd directed the other women and the blue-eyed girl remained. The woman in charge turned to the sheikh and bowed.

The fat man rose, assisted by two of the tribesmen, and Bolan and Muhibbi followed him into the tent, taking seats on mats of camel hair. From behind a curtain to his left Bolan heard whispers and giggles and realized that must have been where the women had gone. The sheikh clapped his hands, shouted "Kamilah!" and the blue-eyed young woman entered the tent with a bowl of steaming water.

Rinsing his right hand, the sheikh passed the bowl to the Executioner before turning to Muhibbi and speaking.

"Sheikh Zarbani regrets he can't speak directly to such an accomplished warrior. He doesn't speak English or Arabic. Only Kirmanji. And he prays that little will be lost through my translation," Muhibbi said.

"Tell the sheikh I understand. Kirmanji? You're Kurds, then?"

Muhibbi smiled. "Perhaps. But the rest of the tribe doesn't believe so. They call themselves Dawasin. In some countries we're known as Yazidis."

Bolan had heard of the Yazidis. Though historians believed them to be of Kurdish ethnic stock, the Yazidis claimed to be a people apart from the human race. According to tradition, they had originated in southern Iraq before migrating to the north and spreading throughout the Mideast.

Kamilah returned, placing another steaming bowl at the sheikh's feet before removing the water. The sheikh lifted the bowl with his left hand, reaching in with his right to remove a huge chunk of breaded meat. Oil dripped from his hand as he extended the bowl to Bolan.

The Executioner turned to Muhibbi as he dipped into the bowl. "You said *they* call themselves Dawasin. And you're a head and a half taller than anybody else in camp. You're Yazidi?"

Muhibbi chuckled, taking the bowl from Bolan. "No. My mother was a settled Kurd from the city of Esfahan in Iran. My father, may his soul rot in hell, was Turkish."

"Your English sounds like you grew up at Oxford. How'd you end up here?"

Muhibbi's smile widened. "Much the same as you. I was returning from England and my car was stopped by these people. I, like yourself, had no money. Or perhaps simply no desire to pay their extortion. I defeated their most able warrior and took his place. I stayed. As you have seen for yourself, once one earns the Yazidis' favor, they are gracious hosts."

Bolan nodded. "Okay. I'll buy it. But this life seems a little remote for a man with your obvious capabilities."

Sadness filled the man's eyes. "It was a simple, remote life-style for which I yearned. Perhaps you'll understand if I tell you of my past. At the age of five my father took me from my mother. I was raised in Syria, not so very far from here in a castle-fortress known as the Eagle's Nest at Alamut."

Bolan felt the chill run down his spine as he recalled his last mission in Syria. He'd destroyed that castle along with the leaders of an ancient cult of hashish-smoking hit men. "The Assassins."

Muhibbi's eyebrows shot up. "You're familiar with them?"

"Let's just say I've heard of them and leave it at that. They're no longer in business."

"Yes. So I understand. The Israeli army learned of their location and erased it from the map."

Bolan saw no purpose in telling him of his involvement. "You were raised as an Assassin, then?"

"Yes," Muhibbi replied. "My father was sent from Alamut to Iran to assist in the underground movement against the Shah. I'm certain he married my mother only to assist his cover. She believed him to be a good man—a warrior for Allah. In truth he was a mercenary—a charlatan and an opportunist. I was five years old when word of *his* father's death reached him. Taking me to be trained and succeed him someday, he returned to the Eagle's Nest to become the Old Man of the Mountain."

"Wait a minute. Sheikh al-Jebal was your father?" Bolan remembered well the pompous oppressor who'd led the Assassins. The world got smaller every minute.

Muhibbi nodded. "He taught me to kill and maim in the name of Allah, but my very soul screamed to me that the things we did were against His will. And I began to notice that those sent on missions rarely returned, while my father's pockets grew heavier."

"So you left Alamut?" Bolan asked. "Your father didn't seem like the type who'd look kindly on defectors—even his son."

Muhibbi shrugged. "It was easy enough. No one expected the son of Sheikh al-Jebal to desert the cause. I spent several years in London and didn't return to Syria until the Assassins had been destroyed."

Bolan stared at the man. The story had the ring of truth, but Sheikh al-Jebal had been a master at brainwashing his recruits. The Executioner had never heard of an Assassin leaving the order voluntarily.

Yet Muhibbi had proved to be an able fighter. He had obviously trained somewhere.

The Executioner's every instinct told him the heart of the man sitting next to him was pure. Perhaps that was what had enabled him to make the break with the cult of demented fanatics.

There was one way to find out. "Take off your tunic, Muhibbi."

"What?"

"Take off your tunic."

A sudden flash of understanding brightened Muhibbi's eyes. "Yes," he said. "You want proof. I don't blame you." Grasping the bottom of the garment with both hands, he lifted it high over his head. There, above his heart, Bolan saw the crescent and star—the brand of those once known as the Assassins. Muhibbi pulled the tunic down. "You're satisfied?"

"Yes, and glad I didn't see that when I had the knife over your head. You should be, too."

Muhibbi laughed. "I am, too."

A tribesman wearing a brightly striped robe and matching keffiyeh entered the tent, carrying a flute. He bowed briefly to the sheikh and then his dissonant, high-pitched notes filled the night as Muhibbi continued.

The desert fighter glanced at the sheikh at his side. "In these people," he said, "I found the simple life for which I longed."

Bolan stared hard at him. "You found a simple life by robbing travelers and killing those who had no money?"

The nomad's skin deepened in color. He shrugged. "Those times are few and far between. These people are poor, and there's contradiction in all life-styles."

"And rationalization," Bolan replied.

"For the most part they're good people. Their loyalty is to the tribe first, then the clan. They don't consider the government in Damascus to be theirs. The Yazidis are very much, I suspect, like my mother's Kurdish ancestors."

Kamilah returned and began gathering the empty bowls. She glanced several times toward Bolan, the spellbinding eyes falling to the ground each time he returned her gaze.

Sheikh Zarbani had continued eating as Muhibbi told his story. He now turned to the tall nomad and spoke in rapid, agitated Kirmanji.

Muhibbi's grin returned. "I'll spare you the names he just called me, but a quick summary would be that he feels left out. The sheikh wishes to know if you're a tourist or on business here in Syria."

"Tell him business."

The Executioner knew that the next question had to be: what kind of business? He considered his options.

It would hardly be wise to walk the streets of Damascus or Beirut, circulating the story that he was looking for the hostages. But he had to start somewhere, and this might be the best opportunity he'd get. Who knew? The nomads might at least have heard *something*.

Sure, they might give him up to the Syrians, but Bolan considered that highly unlikely. He had no trouble believing Muhibbi's statement that the Yazidis held no love for the government. Bolan had never met a tribe of nomads anywhere who stopped to vote and pay taxes.

"Sheikh Zarbani wonders what business you are in."

Bolan turned to face the sheikh directly. "I'm looking for the American hostages held by Hizbullah."

The blood seemed to drain from Muhibbi's face, but then he laughed. "I'll be happy to translate your joke, but then the sheikh will ask me your real business. So—"

"It's no joke. Tell him I'm here to get them out."

Muhibbi hesitated a moment, then turned to the sheikh. The fat man's face revealed no emotion as he was told what Bolan had said.

When Muhibbi finished, Sheikh Zarbani turned to the flute player and barked something in Kirmanji. The man took the instrument from his lips and exited the tent. The sheikh turned back to Bolan, his small black eyes flashing as he spoke.

Muhibbi translated. "The sheikh doubts that even a warrior of your skills can accomplish this mission, but he respects your courage. He's honored by the trust you exhibit in your openness with him."

Kamilah stuck her head through the flap, took a quick look at the sheikh and withdrew.

Bolan looked at Muhibbi. "Ask the sheikh if he knows anything about the hostages' whereabouts."

The fat man listened, shrugged, then began to speak.

Muhibbi translated as he talked. "The sheikh has just returned from a meeting of other Yazidi leaders. Several of our tribes are preparing to move south through Bedouin country, and we must prepare for possible war. But there was a rumor among the sheikhs at the council that may interest you." Muhibbi frowned as he ran a rough napkin across his mouth. "Recently one of the tribes camped near Homs. A house containing an odd group of Arabs was observed. The men had with them a blond woman and others thought to be Westerners. The tribesmen wondered if they might be the American hostages."

Sheikh Zarbani yelled through the tent flap and Kamilah entered, carrying a small branch from the fire. Soft shadows danced across the tent walls as the sheikh filled a giant hookah with tobacco and lit the bowl. He sucked loudly on the stem, his fat cheeks hollowing slightly until smoke rose in a steady stream. He turned back to Muhibbi and spoke again.

"He offers you the use of the pickup truck and three men of your choosing. He regrets that he can't spare more, but problems with the Bedouins may begin at any time."

"Tell him thank you, and I accept. But he may need all the men he has and I don't need three." Bolan stared into Muhibbi's eyes. "The pickup and one interpreter should do."

The nomad smiled and relayed the message. The sheikh puffed thoughtfully on the hookah, then nodded.

6

"Short cut," Muhibbi announced and pulled the pickup off the highway to bounce across the sand. The nomad seemed to know every nook and cranny of the terrain leading south. He'd been pulling off and on the road since sunup.

Bolan glanced ahead, hoping that the man knew the route as well as he claimed. Each tick of the clock brought Sharon Walker closer to death, and the Executioner didn't relish the idea of wasting any of the remaining precious hours stuck in a sand dune.

They should reach Hamah soon before continuing south to Homs. In the meantime, the Executioner could make good use of his time.

Returning his attention to the revolver in his lap, Bolan frowned as he respun the cylinder. The French Lefaucheux wheel gun wasn't smooth. It would have been a shock if it had been—the weapon had to be close to a hundred years old. Using an archaic 12 mm cartridge, the Lefaucheux's operation relied on self-contained "pinfire" cartridges, the firing pin extending at a right angle from the base. It belonged in a case on the wall of a collector, not on the battlefield.

The Lefaucheux and a razor-edged dagger had been parting gifts from the sheikh that morning. The

Executioner was grateful. He needed armament in the worst way. But he'd have preferred something more reliable.

Equipped only with the six hand-loaded rounds that filled the cylinder, he couldn't afford the luxury of a test-fire. And the quick mechanical check he'd just finished left Bolan uneasy. There were dozens of aged parts that could malfunction. Still, it was what he had, and he had to make the best with what was available.

The Executioner shoved the Lefaucheux into his belt, covering the grip with his shirttail, then turned to Muhibbi. "Tell me about the statue outside the sheikh's tent."

Muhibbi grinned. "Ah, yes, Malik Taus. The Peacock Angel. It's the very heart of the Yazidi religion."

"Never heard of it."

"I'm not surprised. The Yazidi faith is kept secret. It includes elements of Christianity, Islam and Judaism as well as certain ancient pagan customs. Malik Taus, the Peacock, was a fallen angel. Much like your Satan."

"He's not 'mine,'" Bolan said.

Muhibbi laughed. "No, I suppose not. But unlike Satan, Malik Taus repented after being cast into hell by Allah. He was restored to His favor. It's by placating the Peacock Angel that the Yazidis receive redemption."

Bolan was curious. "And you've adopted this belief?"

"I'm Muslim. Sunni, I suppose. But to me, Allah, Yahweh, God . . . they're the same."

They pulled back onto the highway as Hamah appeared on the horizon. Bolan watched the green trees, fed with the water of the Orontes River, as they entered the city. They crossed the bridge amid huge wheels that scooped the river's water before spilling it into the ancient stone aqueducts. In the distance he saw the ruins of the ancient quarter, reduced now to rubble by tank and artillery fire.

They sped through the town and continued on toward Homs. Bolan smelled the city before he saw it, the pungent fumes of the town's oil refinery blowing through the Studebaker's open windows.

"As I'm sure you might imagine," Muhibbi said, "many Yazidis have left the nomadic life for the cities. One such man, formerly of our tribe, works near the refinery. We'll see what he knows of the rumor."

The odor of crude oil grew stronger as they entered the city. Muhibbi guided the rattling pickup through the streets to a white concrete office building just outside the refinery gates.

Bolan stayed outside while Muhibbi entered the building and returned moments later with a reed-thin man carrying a clipboard. The man's short-sleeved shirt was open at the neck, and his tie had been pulled loose. He tugged at the collar of his shirt as if it were a noose as he walked to the pickup.

"Meet Thabit," Muhibbi said. Bolan stuck his hand through the truck's open window. He saw Thabit nod as Muhibbi spoke rapidly in Kirmanji.

Thabit scratched hurriedly on the clipboard before ripping the paper away and handing it to Muhibbi. The nomad folded the page and was stuffing it into his tunic as the glass door to the office building swung open. An angry voice shouted through the opening. Thabit nodded nervously, bowed briefly to Muhibbi and hurried back inside.

Muhibbi resumed his place behind the steering wheel and looked at Bolan. Shaking his head, he said, "And you wonder why I choose the life of the Yazidi?"

"Does he know anything?"

"As with most rumors, this one is half true. The house is located not in Homs, but on a mountain road just before Homs Gap, close to the Lebanese border where the Nusayriyah Mountains end."

"How far?"

"Twenty miles, perhaps. Most of it over flatlands."

Bolan settled back in his seat as they drove through the city. He glanced toward Muhibbi, who had grown untypically quiet. In the strained lines of his face, the warrior could see that something was troubling him.

As they turned onto the highway heading east, Muhibbi broke the silence. "We must talk," he said. "There's something you must know. Then you must decide if you wish me to continue with you."

Bolan turned toward him.

"I've told you of my father and mother, but not of my brother." He pulled a date from the sack next to him and popped it nervously into his mouth. "I haven't seen him since I was taken to the Eagle's Nest, but when I returned from England I attempted to contact him." He paused, then continued. "Through an uncle in Esfahan I learned that my mother had died. And that my brother had dropped from sight at the time of the Shah's overthrow."

"Killed?" Bolan asked.

Muhibbi shook his head. "I don't think so. In England I watched the taking of the American embassy on television. One night I looked into the screen and the face of my brother looked back."

Bolan frowned. "But you hadn't seen him since you were five. How could you be sure it was him?"

The nomad sighed. "It was like looking into a mirror."

"Twins?"

"Identical."

"Go on," Bolan said.

Muhibbi took a deep breath and sighed. He turned his eyes from the road and faced the Executioner. "The night I saw him on television…my brother held a gun to the head of one of the American hostages."

The rules of the game kept changing by the minute. Bolan studied the nomad's face. "Anything else?"

"My uncle didn't know where to find him, but Mehmed is rumored to have joined Hizbullah."

As they approached the Gap, the railroad moved closer to the highway, paralleling their path. Bolan leaned back against the seat. So far Muhibbi had appeared to be a confused but honest man. The Executioner couldn't condone the robberies of innocent travelers, but considering the nomad's origins, he'd come a long way down the path from evil to good.

It was possible that Bolan would need the services of an interpreter. Could he trust this man? There was no way to be certain. Not until the nomad had a chance to prove himself. But something inside the Executioner told him that when push came to shove, Muhibbi could be counted on to do the right thing.

He hoped so. Time was running out.

Taking the folded sheet of paper from his tunic, Muhibbi handed it to the Executioner. "You wish me to continue?"

Bolan nodded. He took the roughly scrawled map, navigating Muhibbi through several turns as they ascended a winding road that led up the mountain. Ten minutes later they crested a ridge and saw a one-story frame house in the valley below. He directed the nomad to the side of the road, and Muhibbi reached into the glove compartment, produced a dusty binocular case and pulled the lenses from the case before handing them to his companion.

The Executioner swept the valley below. He found no evidence of occupancy other than a tethered goat chewing on the grass a hundred yards from the house. "Your friend know anything at all besides the location?"

Muhibbi shook his head. "He wouldn't have known that had his brother not visited last week."

Bolan slung the binoculars around his neck. Reaching into his belt, he spun the cylinder of the Lefauncheux once more, grimacing slightly as each chamber ground past the top strap. "Let's take a look."

The grade down to the valley wasn't steep, and it took less than five minutes to descend. Most of the time they were hidden within the thick covering of trees that laced the slope.

The valley still appeared deserted as the two men reached the bottom and stood in the trees twenty yards from the rear of the house. Bolan looked at Muhibbi.

The former Assassin had drawn the curved blade of his scimitar and held it loosely at his side.

Keeping low to the ground, they sprinted to the house, dropping below a back window. Bolan motioned Muhibbi to wait as he made his way around to the front.

Back to the wall, the Executioner drew the Lefauncheux as he rounded the corner to the porch. Holding it close to his side, he paused momentarily to glance through a window next to the door. Flies and cockroaches fed on plates of half-eaten food scattered across the floor. A half-dozen wooden chairs were pushed back from the table in the middle of the room. A backgammon board and round ivory disks littered the table's surface.

Bolan moved to the door and swung it open. He moved swiftly from room to room, the revolver leading the way. Then he drew the curtains in the back bedroom and motioned through the glass for Muhibbi to join him inside.

The steps to the cellar squeaked beneath his feet as he descended. On the damp concrete floor lay two rows of mildewed mattresses, as well as short lengths of rope and balled adhesive tape.

Returning to the main floor, the Executioner found Muhibbi in the rear bedroom. "Look," the nomad said as he dug through a pile of clothes on the carpeted floor. Bolan watched as he opened the front of a woman's jacket to expose the label.

Beverly's Boutique, Wichita Falls, Texas.

Sharon Walker.

Bolan felt his pulse quicken. "Go gas up the truck while I keep searching," he ordered. "We'll need food and water, and better guns—if you know how to get them without attracting attention.''

Muhibbi nodded. ''Where are we going?''

''I'm not sure yet. But I'll know by the time you get back.''

The warrior began digging through the pile. He found both men's and women's clothing with labels ranging from Los Angeles to Washington, D.C.

There remained no doubt. The hostages *had* been here.

Bolan returned to the front room and looked at the rotten food on the plates. They'd been here in the past few days.

Systematically the Executioner searched the premises, making his way around the ground floor before returning to the cellar. He found nothing more of interest except a woman's earring between two of the mattresses.

Bolan returned to the living room and took a seat in one of the chairs around the table. He leaned forward, resting his forehead on crossed arms, and closed his eyes. Hidden somewhere in this house was a clue.

Something, however small it might be, that would point him in the right direction. There had to be. People didn't hurriedly vacate a place where they'd lived for weeks without leaving some evidence as to where they were going.

He'd carefully inspected everything in the house already, which meant just one thing—he'd already seen whatever clue there was. Somewhere, still trapped in his unconscious, floated the memory of something unusual, something not quite as it should be. The

Executioner struggled to raise the elusive, half-formed thought to the surface of his mind.

Beneath his nose he smelled the cool, fresh scent of the cedar table as he racked his brain for the answer. He glanced down at the smooth, unfinished wood of the matching chairs. They were cedar, as well. The evasive idea gradually took shape as the Executioner turned to the end table next to the couch.

Cedar.

He rose and sprinted to the bedroom. The wood of the bed frame looked identical, almost as if it had come from the same tree.

The once plentiful cedar trees of nearby Lebanon were almost extinct. Those that remained were protected by the government. Only a limited number were allowed to be cut each year.

Racing back to the living room, Bolan knelt to inspect the large table closer. The wood was unscarred except for a few places where boots had rested on the edge. The chairs and end tables appeared new, as well.

The Executioner was no expert on furniture. But even to the untrained eye, the pieces scattered throughout the house looked to have come from the same mill. Dropping to the floor, he slid under the large table and finally found the clue he'd been looking for. He couldn't translate the words on the metal plate fastened to the bottom of the table, but it didn't matter. Muhibbi could take care of that when he returned.

What did matter were the two words the Executioner recognized: Tripoli and Bsherri.

Bolan slid from under the table. He found identical tags under the chairs.

The port city of Tripoli, and Bsherri, in the core of the Cedars of Lebanon district.

Bolan dropped to the floor to look for the tag on the end table. He'd started to lean forward when two men with AK-47s burst through the front door.

7

Muhibbi let the Studebaker coast the last hundred yards down the mountain to the trading post. Pulling up to the lone gas pump, he inserted the nozzle into the gas tank. He heard the hum of an engine, and glancing up, saw two hard-looking men climb out of a van.

The two men wore beards and loose muslin vests that fell over their khaki fatigue pants. Looking back at the nozzle in his hand, the nomad watched from the corner of his eye as they entered the store.

Muhibbi shook his head. They'd see many such men this close to Lebanon, men with the frenzied gleam of the spiritual zealot in their eyes, men whose quest to force their own pious dogma on others had gradually driven all reason from their minds.

Muhibbi removed the gas nozzle and hooked it back on the pump, watching the two men close the door behind them. He entered the store as the two men pulled away in the van. He circled the small room, piling nuts, fresh fruits and vegetables into a large basket. In a small, frosty ice box he found a liter container of hummos—chick-peas mashed with sesame oil and garlic—and a large box of lamb cubes, peppers and onions.

At the counter he told the shopkeeper to load three pounds of hot ground lamb into a box with a flat loaf of khobepitaz bread. As the man filled his order, Muhibbi stared through the glass of a case on the counter. Rows of hot, flaky pastry filled with chopped nuts and honey called to him.

While the shopkeeper wrapped the pastries, Muhibbi wondered where the hunt would lead them next. He had no doubt that the man would find something at the house to lead him closer to the hostages. The American was a professional. A professional what he couldn't be certain. CIA? Doubtful. The man had more the bearing of a soldier, a man with a cause he believed in.

In some ways the big man reminded the nomad of the deadly Assassins. The American had the same skills, the same ability to single-mindedly pursue his goals, allowing nothing to stand in his way.

And loyalty. He would be a loyal man to his cause. Like the Assassins, he would lay down his life in a heartbeat for the ideals in which he believed.

But there the similarities came to a grinding halt. His loyalty, while strong, was not blind. He might possess the same deadly skills of warfare that the nomad's father had taught, but the American's abilities were used for good rather than evil.

Muhibbi paid the shopkeeper and returned to the pickup. He wondered briefly if he might find someone nearby with weapons for sale. It would be a dangerous endeavor. A word to the wrong person would have the nervous Syrian border forces on him in a flash.

Returning to Homs made more sense. He could ask Thabit. Muhibbi chuckled. The settled Yazidi reminded him of an American cigarette commercial he had seen frequently in England. "You can take Salem out of the country, but you can't take the country out of Salem."

The same applied to the Yazidi and the desert.

Muhibbi started the engine and headed toward the mountain road. There was no sense in going back to Homs before he checked with him. Perhaps the American had already found the clue he was looking for. If not, he could continue his search while the nomad went looking for armament.

He drove slowly, his mind returning to the fight, and the apparent ease with which the big man had defeated him. True, it had been years since the nomad had trained on a regular basis, but that training had been intense, and as good as any in the world, regardless of the evil motives behind it. It had stuck with him.

A sudden rush of shame filled Muhibbi as he realized for the first time the waste his life had been. The skills he possessed might well have been taught for all the wrong reasons. But they could be put to work for honesty and morality just the same. It didn't matter why he'd mastered the fighting arts originally. What was important was what he did with them now.

The shame dug deeper into Muhibbi's soul as he recalled his past few years with the Yazidis. He'd aided in the robbing of travelers, and after meeting him he could no longer justify the tribe's thievery by the poverty in which they lived.

It had been he who the unfortunate wanderers had been forced to duel when they couldn't pay. True, he'd never killed the men he defeated, sparing them as he had been spared. He'd ended the long tradition of murder by showing mercy.

That thought revived the nomad's spirits slightly. Then the shame returned as he realized he could have changed the Yazidi more—fought from within to bring the tribe to the point where they could exist without stealing and without constant war with neighboring Bedouins.

Suddenly the awareness that he'd passed yet another plateau of his life dawned on him. Like his break with the Assassins, and his decision to return to Syria from England, Muhibbi knew his future was about to take a dramatic turn.

And it was the American he had to thank. Without saying a word, the big man had forced him to open his heart and reach within, searching and then casting out the evil that still remained. Muhibbi had said that his life was no longer his own. But as the man had said, it *was*. What he chose to do with it now would be his decision. Whether he chose to remain with the Yazidi and gradually rid them of the cruel customs in which they still indulged, or offered his services to a government whose aim was to benefit all mankind, Muhibbi knew the rest of his life would be spent in atonement for his early years. He had told the big man that he owed him his life. What he owed him was his soul.

A new joy filled the nomad's heart as he topped the hill that led to the valley and the house. The happiness faded as he spotted the van of the two men he'd

seen at the trading post. Parking the pickup, Muhibbi
got out and drew his scimitar.

THE EXECUTIONER ROLLED away from the table as a
volley of rounds erupted from an AK-47. Drawing the
Lefaucheux from his belt, he thumbed the hammer
and fired from the ground. The recoil stung his hand
as the loose parts of the gun shivered from the explosion.

A huge, empty crater appeared in the forehead of
the first man through the door, then a gush of blood
bubbled forth and dripped onto his beard as he
dropped in his tracks.

Bolan rolled again. More rounds flew from the second man's weapon, gouging fiber from the carpet near
the warrior's former position.

The Executioner cocked the ancient revolver, feeling the cylinder grind as the tired wheel gun rebelled.
He pulled the heavy trigger and fired another 12 mm
round, which drilled into the abdomen of the second
rifleman.

The gunman stared back at him, his eyes widening
as the shock from the round forced his arms to drop.
Still holding the weapon, his eyes never left Bolan
during the split second it took the warrior to cock the
Lefaucheux a third time and aim down the barrel.

Bolan pulled the trigger and heard a sharp, metallic
clink. New hope gleamed in the bearded man's eyes.
Slowly the AK-47 started to rise. The Executioner
pulled futilely at the hammer with his thumb. The
cylinder squealed, started to rotate, then froze. The
gunner grinned as the AK-47 continued upward.

Dropping the useless revolver, Bolan leaped to his feet and vaulted onto the couch. Arms crossed over his forehead, he crashed through the window to the porch outside, followed by the chatter of automatic fire.

Bolan rolled off the porch and drew the dagger from beneath his shirt. Racing to the side of the house, his back against the wall, he peered around the corner as the gunner walked unsteadily through the front door.

The Executioner sprinted along the side of the house to the back. He resumed position, back to the wall, and scanned the area as he waited for the gunman to reappear.

The trees where they'd descended stood twenty yards to his rear. The gunman might round the corner at the side of the house at any moment. If the Executioner was in the open when he did, he'd be little more than a sitting duck.

He had only two choices. He could keep trying to elude his pursuer in the hope that the wound took its toll before the bleeding man cornered him. But one mistake, one wrong move in that deadly game of cat and mouse, and he could forget about reaching the hostages in time.

Or ever.

The other option might be even more risky. He could switch from hunted to hunter, become the stalker himself. But the range of the AK-47 could easily cover the narrow valley, while the dagger's blade extended less than a foot.

Somehow he had to get within reach. The gunman probably wouldn't expect him to try. He was wounded, which would definitely affect his speed, accuracy and judgment. He was most likely dying and probably knew it. That might give Bolan a psychological advantage, as well.

He had to go for it.

Bolan saw the gunman round the corner and ducked back, a 3-round burst streaking past his face. He sprinted to the other side of the house, the stalking man's heavy, wounded breathing loud behind him. As he rounded the corner, he returned the dagger to its sheath. Leaping upward, the Executioner grasped the edge of the roof with both hands and pulled himself up.

Moving silently over the tar shingles, Bolan made his way to the front of the house. One way or the other the man with the AK would return there eventually. The rounds that had barely missed the Executioner were proof that he'd been spotted. The wounded man knew Bolan was circling the house. And unless he missed his guess, the man would reverse directions, hoping to run right into him.

Pressing his body into the shingles, Bolan waited. A moment later he saw the man's face peer around the corner to the front. Seeing nothing, he advanced.

Bolan unsheathed the dagger. He waited as the bleeding man moved nearer, wondering when his gaze would rise to the roof, followed by a deadly burst of automatic fire.

As the man stopped beneath him, Bolan rose to his knees and dived over the edge, the dagger clutched over his head. The gunman looked up in time to take six of the blade's ten inches between his eyes.

The weapon wedged in the man's skull as Bolan fell over the body and rolled to the side. Returning to his feet, he pried the blade from bone and brain, then dragged the body into the living room and dropped it onto the floor. He returned to the porch to retrieve the AK-47.

Searching through the man's clothes, he found keys to the van. As his hands moved under the shirt, Bolan felt a familiar shape. Reaching into the shoulder holster, he produced a Desert Eagle automatic pistol.

The Executioner smiled grimly. He was beginning to feel at home. The .357 Magnum might not be the caliber he'd have asked for, but it would do.

Bolan moved to the other body on the floor. He found thick rolls of both Syrian and Lebanese currency in the fatigues and stuffed them into his pocket.

He'd started to rise when he heard a car pull up outside. The warrior made his way quickly to the window in time to see another man in fatigues exit the vehicle. This guy scanned the front yard as he neared the porch, an Uzi held before him in his hands.

Bolan trained the Desert Eagle on the open doorway. Then, as if from nowhere, Muhibbi appeared next to the terrorist, the scimitar held high over his head. As the startled gunner turned, the blade flashed through the air in a vicious, horizontal stroke.

The new arrival dropped to his knees, staring wild-eyed at the nomad. Then his head toppled from his neck and rolled toward the porch.

Muhibbi burst through the doorway, the scimitar over his head once more. Surveying the scene, he returned his blade to its scabbard. He shook his head and grinned. "It's obvious I can't leave you alone for even a minute, eh?"

The Executioner reached under the table, found the metal tag and ripped it off. "Come here and make yourself useful."

8

Mack Bolan eased the passenger door open, wincing as the rusty hinges screeched through the darkness. Silently he dropped to the ground. Sweat soaked his shirt under the muslin vest. The vest, which had fit the Hizbullah gunner loosely, stretched tightly across the Executioner's shoulders and back, gaping at the chest in front.

"About a mile," Muhibbi whispered to him through the window.

Bolan heard the grinding gears as the pickup pulled away behind him. Hoisting the gunnysack, he held it against his side to cover the distinct contour of the Desert Eagle that pressed through the snug garment. Stepping into the trees, he made his way through the rows of vines.

He'd made good use of the clothes left by the hostages at the house. Stuffed around the disassembled pieces of the Uzi and AK-47s, the clothing broke the outline that the hard steel would have produced within the bag.

Bolan didn't plan on encountering anyone as he made his way to the Lebanese border. But, as always, he'd control every aspect of the mission that was within his power. Nothing was ever gained by intentionally taking chances.

Once again the warrior had run head-on into the same problem that had plagued him crossing into both Turkey and Syria. A problem that had almost resulted in his death back at the house.

Getting weapons across the border.

At first he'd considered breaking down the assault rifles and securing the parts beneath the Studebaker. Risky, but not nearly as risky as entering Lebanon unarmed, hoping he'd find firepower along the way.

Bolan's mind returned briefly to the broken Lefaucheux. He had decent armament now, and he intended to keep it that way.

Hiding the weapons somewhere in the paneling of the van had been another consideration. There was always the chance that the vehicle could be used as a modern-day Trojan Horse. But the tags on the tables and chairs were leading them to Bsherri Furniture in Tripoli. And Tripoli wasn't only second to Beirut in population, but in the terror of ongoing civil war, as well.

In Tripoli he'd encounter terrorists representing all factions of the armed struggles, and the more the Executioner considered it, the more he realized the van was likely to work against him. If it was known to the Maronites, the vehicle might be machine-gunned as they drove through the streets. And if the soldiers of Hizbullah spotted it before he identified *them,* they'd recognize the van.

But not the men driving it.

Bolan's final decision to cross the border clandestinely had come not from the risk of importing firearms, but from another dilemma that might prove equally hazardous. Passports. Muhibbi's British papers shouldn't attract attention, and the nomad would drive the Studebaker across.

For the Executioner the situation was more complex. He still had both the McKay and Harding IDs, but neither would service him under the circumstances. The McKay name had already been burned. Pat Harding's cover said that he was a dentist. American dentists didn't vacation in Lebanon much these days, and if Harding had come to fix teeth, it was doubtful he'd arrive in a broken-down Studebaker with a Yazidi chauffeur.

There had been another option, of course. Both Hizbullah men had carried up-to-date passports. The stamps and dates all appeared to be in order, and the documents hadn't looked like forgeries to the Executioner. One of the bearded men's pictures had even resembled Bolan slightly, and the fact that Bolan was clean-shaven might account for the small discrepancy.

As long as he didn't have to talk.

Nearing the edge of the vineyard through which he traveled, Bolan saw the dark outline of a fence. Someone had posted signs every hundred feet or so along the barrier. Bolan couldn't read them, but he knew what they said—Keep Out.

He scanned up and down the fence. The short barrier ran along a narrow ravine, disappearing into the darkness to his left. A hundred feet to his right it curved out of sight and was lost in the hilly terrain.

It was the right-hand side that concerned the Executioner. Border guards, either Syrian or Lebanese, could appear around the bend at any second.

Bolan breathed shallowly, his ears tuned to the sounds of the countryside. A light wind whistled through the grapevines amid the steady hum of grasshoppers and a woodpecker pecking away in the distance.

Muhibbi had crossed here with the Yazidis several months before. The nomads had cut the fence before driving sheep, goats and camels through the opening. The entire procession had gone unnoticed.

Bolan's eyes strained into the darkness, taking a final look before he stepped from cover. Suddenly the woodpecker's rapid tattoo halted. Turning an abrupt about-face, the Executioner dived back into the vineyard and lay prone on the ground, the Desert Eagle filling his hand.

Thirty seconds later the dark profiles of three men on horseback rounded the curve to his right. Bolan held his breath as they galloped by on the Lebanese side of the fence.

He waited, motionless, as they disappeared into the darkness, then gave them three minutes more. Moving quickly, he sprinted the short distance to the fence and vaulted over.

Muhibbi was waiting when he reached the road, the Studebaker idling while the nomad munched dates from the paper bag. Without speaking, he set the bag on the seat and threw the pickup into gear.

Bolan opened the gunnysack and began to assemble the weapons as they moved down the road to the highway. "Any problems?" he asked Muhibbi.

The nomad shook his head.

The lights of Tripoli appeared on the horizon, and soon they crossed into the city. Seeing the train station, Bolan motioned Muhibbi to the curb and sent him inside to check the phone book.

The Bsherri furniture shop carried the name of a once-famous village in the heart of the Cedars of Lebanon district. The area had supplied lumber for most of the palaces of the ancient kingdoms of the Mideast.

Muhibbi came jogging back, smiling as he crawled behind the wheel. "It's in the town of El Mina," he said. "Two miles from here at the docks on the peninsula." He turned the key in the ignition. "We go there now?"

Bolan nodded.

A VACANT BLOCK separated Bsherri Furniture from the El Mina business district. From the parking lot across the street Bolan had a clear view of the sign that hung from the building's second story. It announced the company name in three languages, including English. Above the sign a row of six windows ran the length of the building's storefront.

Behind those windows the Executioner knew he would find small bedrooms. Tripoli had been an international trading post for over three thousand years, and it wasn't uncommon for businesses of all types to turn their second floors into either hostels or brothels that catered to the sailors in port.

But in those same rooms he might also find the American hostages.

Down the street he could see seamen in the uniforms of several countries, arguing and bargaining with the street merchants for leather goods and jewelry. A lone beggar sat in front of the Bsherri building, his eyes hidden behind cracked sunglasses. One hand held the neck of a stringed instrument, the other a bow, but the man seemed to have no intention of actually playing the instrument. Few people walked the street past the blind man. Even fewer dropped coins into the frazzled basket positioned at his side.

From his seat in the pickup Bolan studied the man. It seemed like a hell of a stupid place to solicit handouts.

Bolan left the Studebaker and motioned toward the blind man. "Keep an eye on him," he instructed Muhibbi.

As he neared the man, Bolan reached casually into his pocket for the roll of Lebanese pounds he'd taken from the Hizbullah gunman. Without breaking stride, he dropped two of the bills, purposely missing the basket. They fell onto the concrete as the Executioner walked past.

Circling the block, Bolan returned to the pickup. "Well?" he asked.

Muhibbi chuckled. "At least he waited until you were out of sight."

The Executioner nodded. "That's enough for me." He slipped off his light jacket, recently purchased in a Western-style department store, looped the shoulder sling of the Uzi around his neck, then replaced the garment. "Let's go," he said.

The nomad closed his all-weather coat over the slung AK-47. "I feel as if I'm about to rob an American bank," he said, grinning.

Bolan saw the "blind" man reach under his jacket as they passed him and neared the front entrance. The black plastic shape of a small radio transmitter appeared. The Executioner turned to Muhibbi and broke into a jog. "He's signaling."

The mixed odors of varnish and sawdust assaulted Bolan's nostrils as he burst through the front door. He jerked free the Desert Eagle, searching the layout on the run. Tables, chairs and other furniture covered the showroom floor. A lone desk faced the back wall next to a staircase leading to the second floor.

A tall, angular man rose from behind the desk, a radio receiver in his hand. The man's startled eyes turned to Bolan as the Executioner reached up to clutch his gaunt throat. "Where are they?" Bolan grated into the frightened face.

At that moment he caught a flicker of movement. Turning, he saw the barrel of an assault rifle poke over the railing that encircled the second floor and sent a double-tap of .357 slugs through the slats of the railing. The rifle dropped, followed a second later by a body that somersaulted onto the showroom floor.

The thin man dived for a desk drawer, but Bolan decked him and sprinted for the stairs. As he reached the first step, he heard a distinctive crack behind him. Glancing over his shoulder, he saw Muhibbi racing toward him, the AK-47 cradled in his arms. The thin man lay in a puddle of blood, the flame-twisted blade of a kris dagger next to him.

A man in a sleeveless undershirt sprang into view at the top of the stairs. Snap-shooting on the run, the Executioner dispatched another set of twin Magnums into the guy's chest, sending him toppling down the steps.

Bolan stepped around the falling body. Behind him he heard Muhibbi curse in Arabic as the nomad encountered the tumbling body.

Reaching the top of the stairs, Bolan saw a flash of steel to his right. He ducked instinctively as the curved blade of a sword streaked overhead.

Straightening as the flashing blade passed out of range, he jammed the muzzle of the Desert Eagle into the swordsman's chest and squeezed the trigger. The man's torso twitched with the concussion, then blood and bone exploded from the crater in the man's back. The sword fell from his hand. Another contact shot sent the gunner crumpling to the floor.

The Executioner shoved the Desert Eagle into his belt and swung the Uzi from under his jacket. At the end of the hall was a closed door. The corridor made a sharp left turn at the door, running along the front of the building. The rooms behind the windows.

The Executioner raced down the hall. A man in flowing robes threw open the door as he neared, and, seeing Bolan, he ducked back inside and extended a pistol around the door frame.

The warrior held the trigger down, sending a long burst of 9 mm slugs through the wall next to the door. Splinters of wood and plaster exploded throughout the hall as the gunman fell into the opening, his robes now wet with blood.

Bolan rushed to the corner, across the hall from the dead man in the doorway. Peering quickly down the corridor to his right, he saw the row of six closed doors. Footsteps sounded behind him, and the Executioner whirled, the Uzi aiming back toward the stairs.

Muhibbi reached the landing and Bolan motioned him forward with the subgun. "Start at the other end. We'll work toward the middle."

The warrior stepped over the robed man's body and into the small room. An iron bed and a wooden bureau stood against the wall in the chamber. Nothing else.

At the end of the hall he heard the sound of a door crashing in, followed by a short burst of gunfire. Bolan rushed out, rounding the corner to the next room. Kicking just below the knob, he sent the paint-chipped door sailing off its hinges. Two men sat upright on the bed, their frightened eyes staring above gags as they struggled against the ropes that bound their wrists.

Bolan turned, stuck his head out the door, then jumped back as a fusillade of bullets from the hall flew past his head. He dived for the bed, grabbed both men around the neck and dragged them to the floor.

More automatic rounds blew through the walls as the gunman near the stairs elected to try the same strategy Bolan had used on the man in the robes. Plaster, wood and paint chips sailed through the room before falling over Bolan and the hostages.

The warrior waited until he heard the bolt of the subgun lock open, then scrambled to his feet. Stepping into the doorway, he stitched the gunman chest to head.

The Executioner dropped the Uzi magazine onto the floor and shoved a fresh load into the grip. Moving to the next room, he kicked the door to find a lone woman, bound as the men, gaping fearfully from the bed.

Sharon Walker? There would be time to find out later.

The next door in line cracked open as Bolan raised his foot to kick, and the barrel of a Makarov automatic poked through the narrow opening. He had to assume there were more bound hostages in the room. If the piercing rounds of the Uzi bore through the gunman's back, the Executioner might easily kill the compatriots he fought to save.

Dropping to his knees, he felt the heat of two rounds blaze overhead as he raised the subgun to a forty-five-degree angle. Showering the doorway left to right, he dived forward, his shoulder forcing the door to swing the rest of the way open.

The rounds had caught the gunman in the shoulders and head. Other than his corpse, the room was empty.

As he hit the fourth door with his shoulder, Bolan heard more gunfire down the hall, followed by a sharp, terrified scream. Muhibbi? There was no time to find out.

The Executioner burst through the opening, Uzi up and ready. The only occupant was a gagged man wearing nothing but olive green paratrooper pants. He struggled to rise as Bolan turned and dashed from the room.

Muhibbi backed into the hall as Bolan turned the corner. Blood had begun to seep through the nomad's coat. He turned to Bolan and said quickly, "It's not bad. One of the swine was hiding under the bed. The bullet just nicked me."

Bolan looked past him into the room. One terrorist lay against the wall below the window. The other was still half under the bed, his dead fingers gripped around the butt of a revolver. An old woman, bound and gagged, sat immobile on the bed.

"Get them untied and ready to move out," Bolan ordered. He raced back to the room of the man in the green paratrooper pants.

Bolan let the Uzi fall to the end of the sling and drew the razor-edged dagger from his belt. Swiftly he sliced the tape that bound the man's ankles and wrists, leaving the gag for the hostage as he bolted back to the woman.

Tears flowed from her eyes as Bolan cut the restraints, and he heard her mumble incoherently as he turned away. An uneasy feeling the warrior couldn't pinpoint swept over him.

As he entered the room holding the two men, Bolan heard a siren in the distance. He rushed to the window. Three blocks away two police cars, lights flashing, led the way from the docks through congested traffic. Four Syrian army jeeps and a troop carrier raced toward the Bsherri building from the opposite direction.

Bolan cut the men's ropes and pulled them to their feet. "Can you walk?" he asked.

"Yes," one of the men replied weakly in a thickly accented voice. "We can run if necessary."

Sprinting back to the hall, Bolan saw Muhibbi leading the elderly woman by the arm. The warrior gathered everyone in the hallway. "Any more hostages?" he asked.

The man in the uniform pants shook his head.

Bolan nodded. "Okay. Army and police are on their way. We've got one chance, and one chance only. Follow my orders to the letter. Everybody got that?"

Five heads nodded in unison. The man who had spoken earlier turned to Bolan. *"Oui,"* he said. "We will do this."

Oui. Not "yes." And the woman muttering in the room as he cut her bonds might have been impossible to understand, but it had been French she'd been speaking.

She wasn't Sharon Walker. She wasn't American.

Bolan glanced over his shoulder. Neither were the rest of them. He had found hostages, all right, but not the American hostages.

Tires screeched to a halt in front of the building, cutting them off from the pickup, which was parked across the street.

The people he now led through the showroom to the production area were French, which meant that somewhere out there, as far away from rescue as they'd been at the beginning of the mission, the Americans still awaited the hangman's rope.

Sharon Walker had two days left to live.

From the front of the building Bolan heard excited voices. He glanced quickly at the tired, fearful eyes of the hostages. The Americans' problems wouldn't seem vitally urgent to them right now.

The time *they* had remaining might be counted in seconds.

9

The manufacturing area was behind the showroom. Making his way around workbenches, power saws and sanders, the Executioner led the way to the rear door. The alley looked clear; the arriving troops hadn't yet had time to set up.

Bolan hustled the hostages through the door. They cut through the lot of a welding shop and crossed the next street to an auto body garage.

The eyes of busy workmen rose briefly as they passed. No one seemed anxious or disturbed by the strange procession, but the Executioner knew they were being watched. As soon as the authorities ascertained what had happened at the Bsherri building, they'd begin canvassing the area. He had to put as much distance as possible between the hostages and their inevitable pursuit.

When they'd covered two blocks, Bolan stopped behind a marine engine repair shop. It was obvious that the weary hostages, weakened by their ordeal, could go no farther. Muhibbi held the elderly woman in his arms, and the younger woman was being led by the man in the military fatigue pants. He appeared stronger than the rest, but even he was showing signs of the strain.

The warrior spotted several large Dumpsters along the edge of the alley. He motioned to Muhibbi, and the nomad began helping the hostages over the sides. "Wait with them," he said. "I'll get the truck."

Bolan swung the Uzi back under his jacket and took off around the corner down the street, sprinting toward the Studebaker. He approached the pickup from the rear, his gaze locked onto the activity across the street. Lebanese police and Syrian soldiers crowded the sidewalk in front of the building. A window blind shot up in the second story, followed by the glass. Bolan saw an excited face lean out and shout orders down to the men below.

The men on the sidewalk raced to their vehicles. Bolan stabbed the key into the ignition, and the Studebaker choked to life.

The Executioner watched the cars and jeeps as he made his way back to the Dumpsters. Several vehicles headed toward the docks, but the majority sped back toward Tripoli, hoping to cut off any escape from the narrow peninsula.

He parked the Studebaker and helped Muhibbi load the young woman and two of the men into the pickup's bed. He carried the old woman to the cab, sliding her in between the driver's seat and the man in the paratrooper pants. Muhibbi swung on board in back.

Bolan glanced toward the man riding shotgun. He'd added an OD green bush hat to his partial uniform sometime before leaving the building. His blood type was stenciled on the left of the brim.

Golani Infantry Brigade. The man was an Israeli soldier. He was damn lucky Hizbullah had let him live.

Bolan threw the truck into gear just as a police car skidded around the corner behind them. Flooring the accelerator, he sped toward the other end of the alley. As the pickup neared the street, another car, tires screeching, spun into the narrow lane to the front of the vehicle.

Cutting the wheel hard right, Bolan jumped the low curb of the alley and raced across the parking lot of a car wash. As he neared the street ahead, he spotted a school bus.

Children screamed in glee as the Executioner hit the brakes, spinning the pickup in a circle. Behind him he heard the young woman shriek as the hostages bounced against the rails of the truck bed. The ancient Studebaker came to a halt, inches from the bus as it passed. The pickup engine coughed twice, then died.

The two police cars, now followed by an army jeep, jumped the curb to the car wash. Bolan twisted the ignition key. Nothing. He turned the key again, and miraculously the engine sprang back to life.

Army jeeps rounded the corners ahead and behind as the Executioner pulled into the street. Vaulting the curb once again, he shot between two houses. More screams came from the back as the pickup crashed through a rickety fence, then downed a clothesline as he burst through to the other side of the block.

Gaining the next street, he raced on as the pursuit cars drew closer, their superior engines taking advantage of the open street. The Executioner heard the sharp crack of revolvers, and a round sailed through the pickup's back window, narrowly missing the old woman and shattering the glass of the windshield. In the side mirror he saw Muhibbi fighting to keep his balance as he knelt over the tailgate and returned fire with the AK-47.

The Executioner leaned out the window and shouted instructions to the nomad. Muhibbi lowered the rifle, took careful aim and fired a single round. The front right tire of the lead car exploded. Almost simultaneously the car fishtailed toward the curb.

Bolan heard the crash as the second police car rear-ended the first. He cut the wheel left at the next intersection and raced along a side street in the residential area.

For the moment the streets were quiet. The warrior knew that would change in a matter of seconds. Two of the pursuit vehicles might be out of commission, but their radios would alert backup as to the direction he had headed. And unless they'd been caught in the accident, too, the two army jeeps would round the block any moment.

The Executioner made a right turn, then a left. At the end of the next block he saw a rickety, run-down house. Grass grew high in the yard, and the open, overhead door gaped in the small garage to the side of the house.

As he slammed on the brakes, Bolan noticed that two of the house's front windows had been shattered. Veering the pickup into the rough gravel driveway, he drove directly into the open garage door. As if reading his mind, Muhibbi leaped from the back and reached up, closing the overhead door and casting the garage into a ghostly twilight.

Suddenly all was quiet except the sirens in the distance and the soft sobs from the rear of the pickup.

Exiting the driver's side, Bolan gently covered the sobbing woman's mouth and whispered, "Quiet, now...quiet."

He felt a faint touch on his arm and looked down to see the elderly woman. The wrinkled face smiled. Stepping back, he lifted her frail body over the rail to the bed. The old woman grasped the hand of the younger one and whispered quietly into her ear.

"The house looks deserted," Bolan told Muhibbi in a hushed voice, "but someone's got to check."

The nomad nodded. Handing the Executioner his AK-47, he drew the scimitar from under his coat.

Bolan shook his head. "If you find anyone, bring him here."

Muhibbi nodded again and returned the sword to his scabbard.

The man with the Golani Infantry hat approached in the semidarkness. "You are American?" he asked.

Bolan nodded.

The infantryman frowned at Muhibbi as the nomad slipped through the side door of the garage. "And him?" he asked.

"It doesn't matter. He's on our side."

The Israeli soldier stiffened, then relaxed and nodded. "I suppose he could have killed us already. If he wanted to."

"Or left you. Hizbullah would have done the job eventually." Bolan saw a meager grin on the man's face. "What detachment are you with?" he asked the Israeli.

The soldier straightened. "Sayeret Golani," he said proudly. "I am Sharabaf, Yitshak...what you would call corporal."

The Executioner looked him up and down, trying to get a reading on the man's physical condition. Sayeret Golani was the Israeli army's primary reconnaissance unit, which was used extensively in counterterrorist operations. Depending on the man's health after captivity—and his experience—he might become invaluable.

The side door opened briefly as Muhibbi returned, carrying an armload of ragged, soiled clothing. He glanced briefly from Sharabaf's pants to his hat, a quick expression of concern flickering in his eyes. He turned toward Bolan and shook his head. "Deserted," he said. "But I found these. Perhaps they'll be of use."

"Good," Bolan said. "I'm going out to look for fresh wheels. Get them dressed as soon as I leave." He paused. "As soon as the police and army realize we're out of sight, they'll start a door-to-door. We've got to be out of here before that happens."

Bolan reached through the window of the Studebaker, pulling the seat forward to reveal the other AK-47 and the rest of the equipment they'd taken from the men at the Gap. He grabbed the assault rifle and handed it to Sharabaf. Turning to Muhibbi, the Executioner jerked his head toward Sharabaf. "Sayeret Golani."

Muhibbi nodded. "I have no problem," he said, reading Bolan's mind again. The nomad turned to the Israeli. "You?"

Sharabaf stared him in the eye. "There's a rumor among my people," he said. "Somewhere out there is one good Arab. One who can be trusted." He paused. "I see that I have found him."

Both men turned to Bolan as a vehicle sped past the garage, siren blaring.

"Okay," Bolan told them. "Stay put and keep them quiet." He glanced at the pickup bed. The younger woman was now leaning against the side, her eyes closed. The elderly woman's arm was wrapped around her shoulders. The two Frenchmen sat against the side of the bed, too, petrified.

Leaning the Uzi against the garage wall, Bolan shoved a fresh clip into the Desert Eagle and slipped through the side door. Two blocks from the garage he spotted what he needed—a mid-sixties Lincoln Continental, white over blue, four-door.

Many such luxury vehicles had been shipped to Lebanon before the civil war had killed the economy. Bolan had already seen what remained of those cars. Dented, in need of paint and in general disrepair, they were still on the roads, dying the same slow death as Lebanon itself. The Lincoln should blend in with them perfectly.

Taking a quick look up and down the street, the Executioner slipped behind the wheel and closed the door behind him. He ducked under the dash just as a Syrian army jeep turned the corner.

Bolan located the necessary wires while the jeep raced past. Uniting them, he heard the Lincoln spring to life.

Sirens still sounded in the distance as he neared the garage. The immediate neighborhood remained quiet. Bolan pulled into the driveway next to the side door. Muhibbi and Sharabaf were already ushering the hostages out when the vehicle came to a stop.

Bolan jumped from the Lincoln and opened the trunk, crowding the two Frenchmen, the younger woman and Sharabaf inside. He slid back behind the wheel as Muhibbi lifted the elderly woman into the front seat between them.

As he backed into the street, the warrior caught sight of three more jeeps parked in the block behind them. Uniformed men on both sides of the narrow street had already begun the door-to-door search.

10

Mehmed Darazi looked up from the book in front of him and glanced at his watch. The luminous face worked only in total darkness, and the oil lamp provided just enough light to render it ineffective. A rush of anxiety hit his chest as he held his wrist closer to the lamp.

Nervously Darazi tapped his pen against the desktop. He hadn't left the cave in two days, and he needed to see the light, needed to see the sun, needed to be reminded that the world of Allah still functioned outside the narrow boundaries of the cave.

Sharp pains struck his abdomen, prompting the Hizbullah leader to realize that confinement wasn't the sole reason for his uneasiness. He forced his eyes back to the open book before him.

His mind stayed in his stomach. Why was it that the only times he felt hunger were when he made a conscious decision to fast? Many days passed during which he became preoccupied and simply forgot to eat. But on the days when he needed a clear mind, when he wished to face the mounting problems without the distraction of food, he often found he could think of nothing else.

In the light of the burning oil lamp, Darazi watched shadows dance across the walls of the small dugout. He'd considered wiring his private room when his subordinates strung the lights in the main cavern and tunnels.

But while they'd been working, and he sat as he did now, reading by the light of the oil lamp, the Hizbullah leader had found he could observe his followers' movements in the shadows cast by the lamp. His surveillance was almost as clear as a closed-circuit screen—and far more effective. A camera would have alerted his men that they were being watched.

Darazi opened the top drawer of his desk and set a date book next to the shortwave radio. He glanced briefly at the entry next to the date, noting the prearranged frequency and the time he was to contact the central control. Again he moved his watch closer to the lamp.

Four minutes. He had to be precise. More than a twenty-second variant, before or after the appointed time, would be considered a breach of security. The Americans at the other holding site would be automatically machine-gunned.

Returning to his book, Darazi again attempted to concentrate. *The Way and the Power: Secrets of Japanese Strategy.* He allowed himself a smile. A book of Japanese thought, written, of course, by an American. It disgusted him to read it, yet he'd found that to defeat one's enemies one must truly know those enemies—regardless of how distasteful that introduction and association might be.

He knew that the difference in thought patterns between the Occidental and Oriental mind had diminished over the years, as the yellow mongrels joined forces with the American whores to subjugate the People of Allah. It was this combined mind-set that he would soon face in battle. He must understand the often ambiguous, often contradictory blend of cultures. He had to fully comprehend the strategies they'd employ if he was to emerge victorious for Islam.

The timer on his wristwatch sounded, warning the Hizbullah leader he had thirty seconds. Carefully tuning the radio, he pressed the button on the microphone and gave the password. The static disappeared as another mike was keyed and the correct response was given.

"Jihad is here," Darazi answered. He replaced the microphone in the bracket mounted on the radio and stood. Excited voices came to him from outside the dugout. He glanced at the shadows on the rock wall, and from far across the main chamber he heard the sounds of a boat arriving. A blurry black silhouette raced toward the dugout entrance.

Harun stepped into view, his weasel-like features driving the hunger from Darazi's stomach. The nauseating man paused to catch his breath. "I have news from Tripoli," he gasped.

Darazi's eyes returned to the book. "Yes?" he asked without interest.

"The French captives have been rescued."

As if a barrel of boiling water had been poured over his head, the terrorist felt the anger flood down his body. "What?" he roared, standing. Without realizing it Darazi reached forward and grasped his puny comrade by the throat. "What did you say?"

Harun tried to speak. The words came out in choked, high-pitched shrieks, and Darazi saw that he was shaking the man's dwarfish frame like a rag doll. He dropped Harun onto the floor and stepped back.

Harun's hands rubbed his throat. "The hostages," he said hoarsely. "The French are gone."

Darazi gripped the edge of the desk. "Who has done this thing?" he demanded.

"It isn't known. Two men attacked the Bsherri building, freeing the prisoners and killing our brothers. They—"

"Two!" he thundered. "Only two men are responsible?"

Harun nodded. "That is the report." He paused, and Darazi could see in the man's frightened eyes that he was debating whether to continue.

The Hizbullah leader knelt before the sitting man, grasping his throat again, lighter this time. "And?"

"There's another report. The house at Homs Gap was attacked. Jabbar, Salim and Zaidi are dead."

Darazi pushed Harun onto his back and rose. He moved silently to the cabinet next to his desk and removed a Russian AK-SU carbine. Unfolding the stock, he hooked it under his armpit as he rammed home a full magazine.

"What will you do?" Harun asked.

The Hizbullah leader didn't answer. Striding from the dugout to the center of the main cavern, he shouted, "Ali! Dawud! Assemble these pigs of Satan against the wall."

He watched as his followers shoved and kicked the hostages to their feet, herding them against the rocks.

Holding the short barrel of the carbine toward them, Darazi walked forward.

The terrorist raised the folding stock to his shoulder and dropped the sights to the forehead of the American banker. He paused, enjoying the look he saw in the man's eyes.

The banker. The defecator. The one who soiled himself as he soiled the world around him in his never-ending lust for money.

Darazi raised the sights slightly and squeezed the trigger, sending a volley of rounds flying over the man's head. The banker fell forward onto the hard stone floor, his hands across the back of his neck.

The other hostages screamed.

"Get him to his feet!" Darazi shouted, and waited while his men jerked the whimpering banker to his feet.

He could kill them. He could kill them all.

And he would. But right now he had to regain control of himself. It would be foolish to waste the bargaining power the Americans still represented.

Handing the carbine to Ali, Darazi stalked to the edge of the rock and stepped down into a boat. "Cover the faces of the swine," he told Dawud. "Keep them where they are until I return."

Darazi started the small motor and guided the boat through the winding tunnels. The sun. He needed to see the sun.

He rounded the last curve, passed the larger boats docked near the entrance and steered into the tiny cove outside. His spirits fell. It was dusk.

Dark clouds began to form over the coastline as he moved out to the open sea. Twisting the throttle, he sped across the water, the salt spray hitting his face, until the lights of the city appeared in the distance. He killed the motor, letting the boat drift with the current, then leaned forward, crossing his arms on his knees.

The Hizbullah leader's mind drifted to the future, to the days of glory yet to come for both himself and Allah.

A sudden surge of guilt crept over him as he realized he should have thought Allah, *then* himself. He dismissed the slip in sequence. In an effort to further know the enemy, he'd read Freud. The Jewish pig would have said his reversed order of thought meant that he placed himself before Allah in importance. But Darazi didn't regard the psychiatrist as anything more than another Western demon.

Allah would always come first in the Hizbullah leader's life, regardless of how he happened to express himself.

Darazi watched the tide roll harder against the distant shore as the clouds continued to darken overhead. When the holy war began in earnest, the first step would be to wrest away what remained of the power held by America, Britain and the other decadent countries of the West. The declining Soviet Union, with its new policy of weakness, would be next.

He watched several blue herons scurry for shore, seeking cover as a light rain began to fall. After the Russians the last segment of jihad would begin. The phase unknown to even the leaders of the nations of Islam, the final stage of the war of which only *he* was aware. The final chapter that Allah had entrusted to him and him alone.

The entire planet would be united in Islam under Allah, and Mehmed Hasan Darazi would rule.

A smile crept over the Hizbullah man's face. Already some of his followers suspected who he truly was. Not a man destined to be an ayatollah, nor even the next successor in the line of Muhammad. He was far more than that.

He, Mehmed Hasan Darazi *was* Muhammad.

Briefly he wondered why Allah had waited so long to return him to earth, then passed the thoughts from his mind. Allah had His plan.

Darazi started the motor and glided through the waves back to the cave, his spirit at peace. As he slowed to enter the cove, he glanced down into the water and saw his reflection in the moonlight.

The serenity vanished as his twin brother looked back at him. Many times over the years he'd wondered about Muhibbi. Was he alive? If he was, he must be somewhere, struggling in the same holy war that Darazi himself fought. Or perhaps his brother had been killed by the enemies of Allah.

If Muhibbi had died, then the blame rested again with the infidels. They would pay for that sin, as well as all their others.

CARS AND TRUCKS were backed up for two blocks on the El Mina side of the bridge. Bolan pulled off the street and sent Muhibbi ahead on foot. Five minutes later the man returned.

"Syrian army," he announced as he slammed the door of the Lincoln. "They're searching every vehicle before it passes."

Bolan frowned. "Any other way across?"

Muhibbi shrugged. "If there is, I'm not familiar with it."

The Executioner started the engine and turned back in the direction they'd come.

"What now?" Muhibbi asked, as Bolan guided the car through the narrow streets.

"The docks."

"They'll be there, too."

Bolan didn't answer. He already knew detachments had been sent to patrol the docks. He'd seen both soldiers and police leave the Bsherri building, headed that way, when he'd returned for the Studebaker. But by far the majority had raced toward the bridge back to Tripoli proper.

Which meant they stood a better chance of escape over the water. Only one problem stood in their way: the Lincoln didn't float.

Bolan's gaze darted up and down the docks as he turned onto the road that ran parallel to the Mediterranean. He drove north along the shore, taking careful note of the scattered police officers and Syrian military personnel who patrolled both on foot and in cars. As the sun set, he passed the loading docks and continued north.

Just before the docks ended, the Lincoln came to a long awning, which provided protection from the elements for small fishing and recreational boats. Past the boats a sandy beach extended before the terrain changed to rock and tall grass. Bolan marked the spot in his memory.

Darkness had fallen by the time he pulled off the road and up a narrow path to the east. Stopping behind a thicket of trees, the Executioner reached up and removed the bulb from the Lincoln's interior light before getting out. He leaned the Uzi, the AK-47s and the extra magazines against a tree and opened the trunk. The two men and young woman stepped stiffly from the trunk. The Israeli got out last.

Bolan secured the trunk, then turned to Sharabaf. "You speak French?"

"Oui," the soldier replied.

The Executioner addressed the group in French. "The bridge is blocked, which means our only chance is by sea. I'm going down to find a boat. I want you to stay here with Muhibbi and Sharabaf until I get back. Any questions?"

The hostages shook their heads.

Muhibbi grabbed his arm. "I'll go with you."

Bolan shook his head. "I've already considered it. One man can steal a boat as easily as two. Besides, Sharabaf's still weak. If anything happens, he'll need your help."

Muhibbi's dark eyes stared back at him.

"If I'm not back in say—" Bolan glanced at his watch "—two hours, you're in charge. Get them over the border however you can. The sheikh said your people are heading south. Make sure the Yazidis get them into Turkey." Bolan turned and started down the path.

The dock had two possible approaches, and the downside of both options lay in the final few steps.

The Executioner had no doubt he could easily make his way along this side of the road to a point directly across from the dock, but if he chose that route, he stood a good chance of being spotted by the light cast by the dock lights.

The alternative was to cross the road here, in the darkness, then follow the high grass to the beach. But from there he'd have to make his way across the sand. While the moon would be the only illumination, the beach spanned a hundred yards of open country.

From somewhere deep within an instinct rose, telling the Executioner to take the beach route. He didn't hesitate. Instinct had kept him alive over the years when common sense and logic would have proved useless. He'd trust instinct again.

Bolan crossed the road and made his way over the rock and grass to the edge of the sand. Squatting in the grass, he saw a lone soldier emerge at the end of the boat walk. The man executed an about-face and retraced his steps into the darkness.

The soldier had obviously been walking assigned rounds. There was no way of ascertaining how long it would be before he'd be back.

Bolan crouched as he sprinted the last hundred yards to the dock. He was ten feet from the awning when the young Syrian soldier rounded the corner in front of him. The young man's mouth dropped open, and his khaki cap fell onto the ground as one hand clawed at the holster on his belt and the other grasped the whistle hanging around his neck.

The Executioner never broke stride. Dropping his left shoulder as he ran, he struck the Syrian squarely in the chest. The soldier gasped, the air rushing from his lungs as he landed on his back. He leaned forward, struggling to sit up, but a hard left cross sent him back onto the boat walk, unconscious.

Bolan scanned the area. There was nowhere to hide the sleeping man. He cupped his hand over his eyes, peering vainly down the line of boats into the darkness. Eventually other guards would notice their companion's absence and come looking for him. That could be an hour from now, or any second.

The Executioner had no intention of finding out. He dragged the soldier to the edge of the dock and tore the man's uniform shirt from his back. Ripping off the sleeves, he used one to tie the soldier's hands behind his back, then fashioned a crude gag with the other. Bolan looped the man's military web belt under his arms and threaded the belt from his pants through the harness to form a sling.

After hanging the crude support over a cleat by the water, he rolled the man over the edge. The leather belt stretched slightly as the soldier's head bobbed under, then his face reemerged, hanging from the harness, two inches above the waterline.

The water chilled Bolan's skin as he lowered himself next to the man. He was about to shove off from the dock when he heard heavy footsteps approaching overhead.

Ducking next to the soldier, Bolan threw an arm around the man's shoulders and pushed inward, forcing him hard against the damp wood of the dock. Then the warrior looked up as the scuffed toes of black combat boots extended over the end of the dock. A voice called out in Arabic.

The Executioner eased the Desert Eagle from under his arm as he heard the rasp of a zipper and the continued muttering of the man on the dock. He pressed the soldier harder against the dock.

A steady stream of urine arced over the Executioner's head, falling into the sea three feet behind him, and the soldier on the dock was still complaining under his breath when the man at Bolan's side opened his eyes. The Executioner turned the young man's face toward his and shoved the Desert Eagle under his chin. The guy got the message.

Finally the splashing stopped and Bolan heard the zipper again. Then the boots moved out of sight and clomped away.

Rapping the Desert Eagle against the soldier's head, the Executioner returned the guy to dreamland.

The hiss of the outgoing tide was the only sound as Bolan sidestroked through the water down the line of boats. He passed a Sabreline 36, then a long Bayliner. Like the Lincoln Continental he'd just abandoned, both vessels were relics of Lebanon's more affluent days.

In the third slip an aging Galaxie tri-hull rose and fell atop the gentle waves. An eighty-five horsepower Chrysler outboard extended from the stern.

The Executioner paused, catching his breath. It would be a little crowded in the sixteen-foot craft, but he doubted any of the host**age**s would demand first-class seats. Just escape.

Slicing the lines with his knife, Bolan pushed the Galaxie slowly from the dock, then let the current pull the boat seaward as he held on to the stern.

The lights behind him were barely visible when Bolan crawled over the rail and started the motor. He piloted the boat slowly along the coast, the moon reflecting off the modest whitecaps his only guide.

As he neared the thicket of trees on the other side of the coastal road, he tapped the front lamp twice. A moment later the Executioner saw the return signal as the Lincoln's headlights flashed through the trees. He killed the ignition and the Galaxie glided quietly to shore.

Across the road he saw six tiny shadows appear from behind the trees. No one spoke as Muhibbi and Sharabaf lifted the two women over the rail while the Frenchmen boarded the other side.

Moonlight danced across the waves as the Executioner piloted the boat north toward Tartus across the Syrian border. He squinted at the hands of his watch as the wind swept sea spray into his eyes.

It was almost midnight. Sharon Walker had a little over forty-eight hours left to live.

11

The Ford LTD left Tartus and continued west, passing cotton and sugar beet fields as Bolan, Muhibbi and the hostages made their way up the winding roads into the mountains.

The temperature dropped sharply as they rose above the low coastal plains, and Bolan leaned forward, switching on the car heater. He checked the gas tank.

Half-empty, to the pessimist. Half-full, the optimist would say.

At this point the Executioner wasn't sure which of those two categories he fit into.

After picking up Muhibbi and the hostages, the rest of the trip on board the Galaxie had gone without incident. From the sea Bolan had spotted Tartus Castle and returned the party to shore just outside the Syrian city. Hiding the boat in a grove of tall cane stalks, he'd again left the hostages in Sharabaf's care while he and Muhibbi made their way into town.

While Bolan procured the LTD from a parking lot, the nomad had telephoned Homs, learning from Thabit that the Yazidi advance party had already arrived in the mountains just to the west. They were setting up camp now as they awaited the arrival of the herds and the rest of the tribe.

Next to him in the front seat Bolan heard Cecile begin to snore. He laughed silently as the elderly Frenchwoman's head leaned harder into his shoulder. Cecile had held up admirably during the flight from Tripoli, but wear and tear had finally caught up to her. Leaning back under a rotting, mildewed shawl Muhibbi had found in the deserted house, she'd nodded off as soon as they'd gotten on the road.

Bolan glanced into the back seat. The two Frenchmen and the younger woman were asleep, as well.

On Cecile's other side Muhibbi shifted position, scanned the sleeping passengers, then looked at the Executioner. "We're back where we began," he whispered.

Bolan kept his voice low. "Worse. Time's running out."

Cecile opened her eyes and sat up in the seat, staring blankly at the windshield.

"We've got to find another lead, Muhibbi," Bolan said. "I'm not giving up. But for the moment I don't have idea one as to where to begin."

Cecile looked up and said, *"S'il vous plaît."*

Bolan glanced down at the plucky little woman. "Yes?"

Cecile continued in French. "I do not speak English well, but I have heard you both converse in my language." She paused. "In France it is considered very bad manners to speak in a language that your guests do not understand."

Bolan smiled, switching to French. "I was saying that we've got to locate the American hostages—fast—and I'm not sure where to start."

Cecile shrugged her frail shoulders. "Beirut."

"Beirut?" Muhibbi asked. "Why?"

"Because that is where they are being held."

Bolan turned to her again. "How do you know?"

Cecile blew air between her closed teeth. "In Tripoli I heard the devils talking."

The Executioner frowned. "You speak Farsi?"

"Fluently. But our captors did not know this. My husband, may his soul rest in peace, was a diplomat in Tehran for ten years." Cecile reached up, grasping the crucifix around her neck. "I did not feel it wise to share *that* knowledge, either."

Bolan left the main road and turned onto a narrow blacktop. They were far above the lowlands now, and if Thabit's directions were accurate, they should soon see the Yazidi camp.

"What else did you overhear?" Bolan asked.

"An American woman is the next to be hanged."

"Yes. They've made that public. Anything about where they're being held?"

The old woman nodded. "They have been divided and are at two locations. At least that is what I gathered." She turned, smiling into the Executioner's eyes. "Often they said the word *Damascus*. It is possible they meant the city. But somehow I do not think so."

"Why not?"

"It is hard to explain. The context in which they used the word, I suppose. I am certain the Americans are in Beirut—at least some of them. One night, when they believed we were asleep, one of the terrorists actually said 'They are still in Beirut.' I took this to mean the Americans. Then his friend agreed, calling the same place Damascus. The first man laughed, saying it was where the infidels would be least likely to look and that a rescue team would search the museum first.''

"Any idea what that meant?" Bolan asked.

Cecile shook her head.

Beirut. Damascus. Bolan ran the seemingly contradictory scraps of information through his mind. If the hostages had been divided, one group could have remained in Lebanon while the other was sent to the Syrian capital. It made sense for security reasons.

But if the Frenchwoman was right, and Damascus didn't mean the Syrian capital, then it had to mean something else, something he had to figure out quickly. It could be the key that unlocked the mystery of the other fragment of information the woman had overheard.

Where the infidels are least likely to look.

And what did "the museum" mean?

"There is one thing," Cecile said, breaking into his thoughts. "On another occasion I overheard one man say that if the phone call was not received on time, twenty seconds later, they would all be killed."

"What call?" Bolan asked. "That Israel had freed the Hizbullah sheikh? That their demands had been met?"

Cecile shrugged. "I am sorry."

Over a small rise in the road, in the narrow slope of a valley between two mountains, Bolan saw several men raising a tall tent post. A large bonfire flamed to the side, the charred carcass of a lamb rotating on a spit above it. As they neared, Sheikh Zarbani's bloated form appeared atop a camel. The sheikh's plump arms waved wildly in the air as he roared orders to the workmen.

Bolan slowed as they neared. He saw the men secure the tent post and turn toward the car, their hands dropping to weapons on their belts.

Muhibbi opened his door, and Bolan felt the cold bite as the mountain wind swept through the car. The Yazidi men smiled, replacing their firearms and swords as they recognized Muhibbi.

Two of the tribesmen helped Sheikh Zarbani dismount. The sheikh's fleshy lips fell open in shock as the French hostages stepped out of the car. A broad smile replaced his surprise as he embraced Muhibbi, speaking rapidly in Kirmanji.

Muhibbi shook his head, then both men turned to Bolan. "He wants to know if we were successful."

"Not exactly," Bolan replied. "These aren't the people I came looking for. But they need your help."

Muhibbi translated as Bolan explained the situation with the French hostages. The sheikh smiled and nodded, agreeing to see them safely into Turkey as soon as possible.

Bolan turned back to the car. The sheikh shouted after him.

"Sheikh Zarbani wishes us to stay for a meal. They have just butchered two sheep, and there's far more than they can eat."

Bolan glanced at the corpulent nomad leader. He doubted that was true. "Tell him thanks, but there's no time." The Executioner opened the door and slid behind the wheel.

Sharabaf walked to the driver's side as Bolan stuck the key in the ignition, and he rolled down the window as Sharabaf spoke. "I shall go with you," the Israeli offered.

The Executioner studied the man, who was worn and emaciated after months of captivity. "No," he said gently. "Go with them. They need you."

Sheikh Zarbani approached the car, carrying a large goatskin pouch. Without speaking he extended it through the window. The fragrant odor of grilled mutton and spicy rice wafted through the car as Bolan set it on the seat. Turning the car around, he started back down the mountain road.

AS THEY APPROACHED the cane grove, Bolan detected movement through the stalks. Nearing, he made out the ragged form of a man sitting behind the wheel of the Galaxie. An overturned canvas bag, freshly picked cotton spilling from its mouth, lay half in the water by the boat.

The cotton farmer drew a short dagger as Bolan and Muhibbi stepped out of the cane. The nomad's hand fell to his scimitar, but Bolan reached out, stopping him. "Ask him what he's doing."

Muhibbi let his hand drop as he spoke rapidly in an Arabic dialect. The man answered and Muhibbi translated. "He's found the boat, and he's afraid we'll steal it from him."

Bolan surveyed the man's threadbare clothing. He wore a frayed Western sport coat above the same type of baggy pantaloons as Muhibbi. A soiled and torn keffiyeh covered his head. The farmer smiled nervously and glanced down at the boat. A grim expression of determination replaced the smile as he spoke again.

Muhibbi turned to the Executioner, unsheathing his sword. "He's prepared to fight to the death."

Bolan shook his head. "Ask him what use a cotton farmer has for a boat?"

The farmer spoke rapidly, his hands moving in the air.

"If he finds a buyer, he can feed his family for a month."

Bolan reached into his pocket and withdrew a handful of Syrian bills. "Tell him he's found a buyer." The Executioner extended the notes toward the man.

The cotton farmer's eyes widened, then he frowned. Stepping out of the boat, he kept the dagger in front of him. His other hand reached forward apprehensively. Taking the money from the Executioner, he backed cautiously away. Ignoring the bag of cotton, he disappeared through the stalks.

High winds blew over the Mediterranean as they made their way from shore, careful to get out of sight over the horizon before heading back, parallel to the coast.

The Executioner gazed at the oncoming waves as he guided the Galaxie toward Lebanon. Holding the course due south, he estimated the time the trip north had taken the night before, then turned the boat east and headed back toward the coast.

The skyline of Tripoli rose out of the waves. Pulling to shore along the empty beach across the road from the Lincoln, Bolan and Muhibbi quit the Galaxie and sprinted toward the trees.

The nomad stretched out in the back seat of the vehicle, intent on catching a catnap. He'd suffered a bout of seasickness during the trip and needed time to recover.

The Executioner pushed the Lincoln along the winding coastal road for half an hour before waking Muhibbi. The nomad's red eyes blinked repeatedly as he forced himself back to consciousness. Sliding into the back seat, Bolan closed his eyes.

Beirut.

Damascus.

Where the infidels are least likely to look—they'll look in the museum first.

What did it all mean?

Far in the distance the battered skeleton of a city in its death throes appeared. As they drew closer, Bolan saw the ruins and rubble of the once-thriving "Gem of the East." He ordered Muhibbi to the side of the road and took the wheel.

"I seem to be asking you this a lot," Muhibbi said, "but where do we go from here?"

"The American University," Bolan answered. He saw the nomad's brows knit. "I need someone who's familiar with the city, someone who knows the ins and outs and all the subtle peculiarities of the culture that may be wrapped up in this puzzle."

"And someone we can trust," Muhibbi added.

"That goes without saying. And the university's the best place to start."

The road bent westward, following the coast onto a broad peninsula as they made their way through Beirut's Muslim section. They passed the port area, driving slowly through the bombed-out rubble of Lebanon's downtown no-man's-land.

Bolan nodded as he maneuvered the Lincoln around huge chunks of concrete and the ash-ridden remnants of burned lumber. The debris had been swept to the sides of the street, clearing just enough room for pedestrians and a double lane of traffic.

He shook his head as the Green Line appeared ahead. Christianity and Islam both proclaimed peace and brotherly love, but certain factions of the two faiths had a strange method of achieving that objective.

Sudden thunder boomed in the street, and glass shrapnel from the Lincoln's windows showered across the front seat. Bolan felt the steering wheel wrenched from his grasp as the car spun out of control, the metal rims of the wheels knifing through blown rubber to send sparks sailing through the air.

The Executioner fought to regain control as the Lincoln skidded over the sidewalk and rebounded off the brick wall of a deserted building. Easing his foot onto the brake, he brought the car to a halt amid a pile of rubble and dust.

Bolan and Muhibbi leaped from the stalled vehicle as a second bomb exploded across the street, sending concrete, wood and smoke mushrooming overhead. The Executioner's hand shot reflexively under his jacket, his fingers encircling the grip of the Desert Eagle.

No. He couldn't risk exposure. Not at this point. Besides, who would he fire at? He had no definable target.

Shots rang out, and Bolan glanced quickly toward the Lincoln's trunk. A giant mass of brick and concrete rocked slowly back and forth across the rear of the car, caving in the trunk and blocking access to the assault rifles and Uzi.

A short burst of automatic gunfire erupted, and a smoking pattern of holes appeared in the fender near the Executioner. Dropping to the street, he crawled under the vehicle and came up in a crouch behind the engine block on the other side. He scanned the area, looking for Muhibbi.

The Executioner heard a shrill whistle over the gunfire and turned to see the nomad beckoning him from behind. Muhibbi had taken refuge behind the stacked sandbags that encircled a transit station. Dropping prone once more, Bolan crawled toward the bags, estimating the sniper's angle of trajectory before he'd reappear in the man's sights.

He'd returned to his feet and was sprinting toward the station when the shots resumed, skimming past his feet before plunking dully into the sandbags.

Bolan dived over the barricade, taking cover next to Muhibbi. Behind him he saw the transit station proprietor frantically rolling down the iron shutters over the windows.

The Executioner motioned to a narrow alley leading between the station and the next building. "Let's go."

The two men scrambled to their feet and sprinted to the narrow passage, tiny grains of sand and concrete raining down onto their shoulders as more rounds ricocheted off the buildings overhead. They rounded the corner and raced down the alley to the street behind the building.

Away from the firing now, Bolan and Muhibbi slowed to a jog. Ahead, the tall trees announced the hotel district along the shore.

They flagged a cab and passed the hotels, the gunfire behind them fading as they left the combat zone of downtown Beirut.

12

Sporadic gunfire still sounded in the distance as Bolan and Muhibbi walked to the door at the end of the hallway. The words on the smoky glass read: History, Leon W. Snodgrass, Ph.D. Bolan knocked lightly on the glass.

"Come in," a gravelly voice from inside said.

The Executioner opened the door. Behind the desk at the far end of the office sat a man with snow-white hair and silver-rimmed glasses. Deep channels cut through the tanned skin of his forehead above innumerable crow's-feet at the corners of both eyes.

The man looked like a cat poised to move quickly. Palm down on the desk in front of him, his left hand pushed hard against the surface, ready to spring him to his feet. His other hand was out of sight under the desk in the chair well. The upper right-hand drawer of the desk lay open. It didn't take a genius to figure out why.

Snodgrass's tired, bloodshot eyes registered concern as Bolan and Muhibbi entered the office. But the Executioner could see that actual fear had long ago been washed from the faded blue orbs. On the desk ice melted in an empty highball glass next to a half-empty bottle of Scotch whiskey.

"What can I do for you?" the man asked.

"You can put the gun up for one thing." Bolan glanced toward the window as more muffled shots sounded in the distance. "It's no mystery why you'd want protection, but you don't need it from us."

The crow's-feet deepened as Snodgrass's eyes narrowed slightly, then a cocked Government Model .45 appeared over the desk. The click of the safety echoed throughout the office before he set the gun on the desk. The professor's white hair flopped slightly as he nodded toward the same window. "You can't get too careful around here," he said. "I'm Leon Snodgrass. You'll understand if I don't shake hands. Just yet."

The Executioner nodded. "Mike McKay." He noted the soiled white shirt the professor wore, stained a light tan with sweat. The knot of Snodgrass's frayed tie had been yanked down to the third button of his shirt and hung askew to the left.

"Dr. Snodgrass," Bolan began, "I've got some questions to ask and I don't have a lot of time. Briefly let me tell you I'm an American, and I'm looking for American hostages held by Hizbullah and this man's helping me."

"CIA?" Snodgrass asked.

"No."

"Who, then?"

"Does it matter?"

Snodgrass shrugged. "I'm a former Marine. So was my son." He glanced at a framed photograph on the wall.

Bolan's eyes followed and saw a smiling young Marine in dress uniform.

"He was stationed here," the old man continued, "at Marine HQ when Islamic Jihad bombed it in 1983." Bolan saw the man's eyes narrow again, and a vicious snarl twisted Snodgrass's lips. "John volunteered for this duty to be close to me. It's my fault he's dead."

"Dr. Snodgrass—"

"Call me Leon." The pale eyes returned to the Executioner's. "I'm sorry. I'm getting old and I drift sometimes. But I can't help feeling—"

Bolan shook his head. "The parents of 240 other Marines probably feel the same in one way or another. None of you should. The only people who are responsible are the terrorists who planned and executed the bombing. The same kind of savages who're about to execute fifteen more innocent Americans if I don't get to them first."

Snodgrass dropped the .45 into the drawer and closed it. "How can I help?"

"We're running short on time. I've got several scraps of information, and I'm hoping you can help me put them into perspective." He repeated the assorted pieces of the puzzle while the professor listened, frowning.

"Damascus may be easier than you think," Snodgrass said when Bolan had finished. "Damascus Road separates the Muslim and Christian sections in the north part of the city."

"The Green Line?"

"Yes, as far south as Yafi Avenue. Then the road branches east."

Bolan nodded. "It sounds reasonable. One of the locations might be referred to as Damascus if it's on the road. If the other pieces fit. What about museums?"

"Like any capital city, Beirut's got its share."

"Any along Damascus Road?"

Snodgrass frowned. "Several." He rose and walked to a filing cabinet across the room. Rummaging through the bottom drawer, he produced a wrinkled, soiled brochure. "Yes. *Beirut: Points of Interest.* We used to give this to new students." He paused, his mind drifting again. "That seems like a long time ago." He returned to his chair behind his desk.

Bolan reached out, extending his hand. "Thank you, Doctor. You may have been more help than you think."

The wrinkled historian smiled weakly as they shook hands. "There was a time, McKay, when I thought I'd find the sons of bitches who killed my son. Planned to kill them myself." The old man's shoulders slumped slowly forward. "But the fight's long gone out of me." Opening the top drawer again, he pulled out the .45 and four loaded magazines. "You may need this." Bolan started to speak, but the old man raised a hand. "Don't worry about me," he said. "I've got two .38s at the house. I can bring one down here."

Bolan took the gun and handed it to Muhibbi.

"You'll need transport." Snodgrass reached into his pant pocket and removed several keys, then flipped the ring to Bolan. "White Buick," he said. "West parking lot."

Bolan nodded. "Thanks again. We'll try to get it back to you, but I can't promise anything." He turned toward the door.

"Yes, you can," Snodgrass said, a new fire lighting up the faded eyes. "I don't give a damn about the car. But you can promise me something."

Bolan turned back to him.

"You can promise me you'll find the hostages and kill the bastards who are holding them." Snodgrass paused, then pointed at Muhibbi, who still held the .45. "And if you can," he whispered, "do it with my son's gun."

BOLAN SHIFTED, trying to get comfortable. The springs poking into his thighs had long ago worn through the vinyl seat covers, then sometime later they'd penetrated the black masking tape Snodgrass had used to repair the holes.

Bolan heard Muhibbi grunt in disgust as the flimsy cloth covering the car's ceiling fell over his head. Dislodging one of the dozen or so thumbtacks scattered across the roof, the nomad grasped a handful of the dangling material and jabbed the tack through to the foam rubber. "This is worse than the pickup," he complained.

Bolan nodded. The condition of the Buick was an indication of the history professor's emotional decay. Leon Snodgrass had lost more than his son in the suicide bombing on Marine Headquarters in Lebanon. He'd lost his pride, as well.

Bolan turned the car south onto Damascus Road, scanning both the Christian and Muslim sides. The shooting had all but stopped, though lone rounds periodically exploded in the distance.

"Ahead," Muhibbi said as they passed the Place des Martyrs, "is the Museum of Phoenician Coins and Pottery."

Bolan slowed the Buick. On the right-hand side of the road the empty cavity of a gutted building stared at them as they passed. "Scratch that one," he said.

According to the brochure Snodgrass had provided, three more museums lay along Damascus Road before the Green Line curved west. Bolan kept a steady pace past another burned-out ruin, then slowed at the Lebanese Museum of Agriculture. On the Christian side of the street the museum seemed as busy as one would expect in a city where survival had taken precedence over tourism.

"We'll keep it in mind. What's next?"

Muhibbi squinted at the brochure, the fading light of the descending sun making it difficult to read. "Abdullah Yafi Museum of Art," he said. "At the divide, where the road intersects with Yafi Avenue. It's just across the street in the Muslim sector."

As they passed Abdullah Yafi Avenue, Bolan saw the museum, a half block east across the Green Line. He pulled to a stop next to a small bed-and-breakfast hotel. Across the street to the south sat a Christian church. He killed the ignition and sat back against the seat.

"What now?" Muhibbi asked.

"We watch."

The front windows of the Yafi museum had been replaced with jagged sheets of plywood. From where they sat Bolan could see the padlock securing both ends of the chain that wound through the bar locks on the steel doors. The street in front was deserted except for an old man who was digging through the trash cans to the side of the building, stopping periodically to eat whatever he'd found.

They'd been there close to an hour when the panel truck arrived. A hard-looking Arab got out, carrying a grocery bag. When he reached the door, he removed a key, unlocked the padlock and disappeared inside.

Muhibbi pointed at the Arabic letters on the side of the panel truck. "Beirut Foods," he said, translating. "More or less."

The Executioner nodded. But why were groceries being delivered to a vacant museum?

The Arab reappeared, locked the door and returned to the truck. Bolan reached forward, twisting the key in the ignition as the panel truck crossed into the Christian sector. He killed the engine and sank below the dashboard, Muhibbi following his lead. The truck came to an abrupt halt across the street at the church.

Bolan peered over the dash as the delivery man got out and saw him heft three heavy sacks. He was met at the door by a slender man dressed in the black cassock of a Maronite priest.

Bolan and Muhibbi watched as the two men made four more trips to the truck, each time carrying three sacks of food apiece into the church.

Something was definitely wrong. Did the church serve as a refuge for the hungry and homeless victims of the civil war? If so, why hadn't they seen any activity around the building? The priest appeared to be alone in the building, but the panel truck had just delivered enough food to feed an army.

Sudden realization struck the Executioner like a lightning bolt between the eyes. That was exactly what they were doing. They were delivering provisions for an army.

An army of terrorists.

A rescue team would check the museum first. Right. And when they did, they'd find no one but a lookout who would quickly alert the guards of the real location that a rescue attempt had been launched.

Where *was* the real location?

Where the infidels would be least likely to look.

A Christian church.

It all fit. *Beirut. Damascus Road. They'll look in the museum first.* The panel truck undoubtedly had dozens of stops on its route, each phony and each prepared to notify the hostage location at the slightest sign of trouble.

Bolan was roused from his thoughts by Muhibbi. "Are you thinking what I'm thinking?"

The Executioner watched the Arab leave the church and speed away in the panel truck. "I am," he said. He glanced quickly at the small hotel to his right. "But there's only one way to find out for sure."

13

In the dim light from the corner streetlamp, Bolan studied the cross at the top of the Maronite church. The symbol of Christianity stretched from the steeple toward the sky, its dark silhouette outlined by the moon. From their second-story room across the street he could see one side of the church as well as the main entrance facing the small hotel.

From the street below Bolan heard a shout, then laughter. He glanced a block to the east, across the Green Line to the Muslim sector. In front of the Abdullah Yafi Museum bands of teenage boys roamed the streets, stopping occasionally in the darkness to engage in the mock fights of oncoming manhood.

Earlier, before nightfall, Bolan had studied the grounds around the church. The ancient building stood on the corner of Damascus Road and Avenue Abdullah Yafi, a one-story office building flanking its other side. A narrow alley ran behind the building, debris from the frequent violent outbreaks overflowing the trash cans and stacked along the sides.

A row of basement windows started halfway down the side of the church to the rear, and unless the Executioner missed his guess, they extended around the corner to the back of the building, as well.

Bolan walked to his bed and picked up his Desert Eagle and his knife. Then, on second thought, he dropped the Israeli automatic back onto the mattress before strapping the knife to his belt.

Muhibbi frowned. "What are you doing?"

"This is recon only," Bolan told him. "No noise."

Muhibbi pulled the .45 from his belt and laid it next to the .357. "We go now?"

"Not we. Me."

Muhibbi stood. "But—"

Bolan raised a hand. "There's no place for you tonight. Two men are more than twice as easy to spot as one."

"But we can recon, as you say, then strike immediately," Muhibbi argued.

Bolan shook his head. "The hostages aren't going to be right inside the door. We've got to know the layout of the building, find out exactly where they are. If the terrorists hear us coming, we'll find nothing but dead bodies."

Muhibbi looked disappointed. "Besides," he went on, "if anything happens to me, I'm counting on you to get them out."

A new pride washed over Muhibbi's face, then he shook his head. "Well, as you Americans say, 'shit.'"

"Don't worry. If I'm right, you'll see plenty of action in the morning."

Bolan closed the door behind him and descended the stairs. The young olive-skinned girl who'd checked them in earlier sat behind the glass in an archaic wooden phone booth by the front door. She shot him a smile as he crossed the lobby to the street.

The Executioner turned right at the sidewalk and strolled casually down the street into the Christian sector. Two blocks down he crossed at the corner, then cut down the alley leading back to the church.

Stopping behind the darkened office complex, the Executioner peered around the corner. A white van, similar to the one they'd seen at Homs Gap, and two small Hondas were parked in the spaces behind the church. As he'd guessed, more sunken windows ran the side next to the office building and along the back.

Bolan glanced both ways, then crept noiselessly between the vehicles to the closest window well. Silently he dropped out of sight.

The distant sound of traffic on Damascus Road was the only sound. Bolan slipped his knife from under his jacket and looked through the smudged glass. A large, shallow basement, apparently used as a storage room, extended halfway to the front of the building. Faint light trickled through the windows facing Damascus Road, casting shadows over boxes and chairs that were piled from floor to ceiling.

Gently the Executioner reached out and grasped the window latch. Locked. The glass would break easily enough, but even though the basement looked deserted, there was always the chance that someone occupied a room nearby. He had no desire to announce his presence. Even if he wasn't heard, there remained the distinct possibility that the broken window would be discovered before he and Muhibbi could return in the morning.

Bolan studied the latch on the inside of the window, which was a simple trip catch. He pulled gently, and the window moved forward a quarter of an inch.

Sliding the blade between the glass and the frame, he flipped the catch and nudged the window outward. A moment later he was inside.

Moving quietly through the darkness, Bolan stopped to inspect one of the piles of stacked boxes. Canned goods—fruit, vegetables and meat. Again enough to feed an army. Hizbullah could hold up inside the church for weeks in the event that the delivery truck was exposed.

Bolan made his way cautiously up the stairs, pausing to listen each time the aged wood creaked beneath his weight. Soft light fell down the stairs from above, growing brighter as he came to a landing. He paused at the open doorway at the top. A blank wall faced him on the other side of a hallway. Dropping to his knees, he let his eyes adjust to the light, then glanced around the corner.

The church sanctuary stood to his right at the front of the building. The other end of the hall dead-ended at a swinging door twenty feet to his left. The Executioner rose to his feet and was about to step forward when the sudden sound of approaching footsteps forced him back into the shadows.

Pressing his back against the wall of the stairwell, Bolan watched as the priest, a PM-63 9 mm machine pistol slung over his cassock, hurried past the doorway from the sanctuary. The Executioner waited until he heard the swinging door open and close, then moved silently down the hall to the sanctuary.

Candles burned on the dais, illuminating the face of Christ on the cross. Directly over Bolan's head, the sculpted forms of winged demons threatened to descend from the ceiling to grasp their unfortunate victims in their claws and carry them down to hell.

Bolan knew there were demons in this church, all right, but they didn't have wings. They had PM-63s and assault rifles.

And American hostages.

Next to the confessional at the rear of the sanctuary, Bolan spotted a closed door. Crossing quickly, he peered behind the curtains in the small booth, then moved on to the door.

The Executioner's foot slipped beneath him as he neared the door. Kneeling, he felt the small puddles of water on the stone floor. He pressed his ear against the grainy wood. From somewhere far away came the steady drone of moving water.

The door was locked. Bolan drew his knife, used it to jimmy the bolt, then slowly he opened the door. He stepped through to the top of a darkened stairway. Thirty feet below he could see light reflecting off the water that ran in a steady current along a stone walkway.

Catacombs?

Descending as quietly as possible, he felt the temperature drop sharply as he neared the bottom. He paused on the last step and scanned the paths ahead.

The tunnel led from the stairs to a small fork, then branched right and left. Stepping down into the water, Bolan felt the steady current of the cool water against his ankles. Suspended from ceiling beams, oil lamps lighted both shafts. Alcoves had been carved into the walls, and he could see the remains of ancient coffins resting in the recesses.

Voices came from the right branch of the tunnel. Bolan followed the sounds, wading as quietly as possible along the corridor. He slowed as he neared a corner.

The voices became audible. Carefully he peered around the stone. An angry voice screamed in Farsi, and a slap was followed by a moan.

A soft voice whimpered, "Please..."

The accent was unmistakably southwest United States.

Sharon Walker?

The Executioner felt the anger rise in his chest. He fought the impulse to rush to the end of the watery corridor, to attack before any other pain could be inflicted on the hostages.

But the water slapped loudly with every step he took, echoing off the narrow walls of the catacombs. He risked exposure with every movement. And if he was discovered, his knife wouldn't go far in freeing the hostages.

He'd gotten what he'd come for, learned what he needed to know. The Americans *were* here. At least some of them. Attacking now, unarmed, would be the height of futility and foolishness. Bolan had come a long way, searching for his fellow Americans, and he wasn't about to blow it now and get them killed in a half-baked rescue attempt.

What he had to do now was return to the room, rearm and send Muhibbi to check out the left branch of the catacombs while he made his way down this one.

Bolan abruptly turned back toward the stairs. Climbing quickly to the sanctuary, he cracked the door and peered through the opening. The bogus priest stood near the dais, and the Executioner waited while the impostor blew out the candles before disappearing down the hallway once more.

Bolan crept softly across the sanctuary. He was ten feet from the door when he heard the footsteps, and suddenly the priest stood framed in the doorway. The man snatched at the machine pistol on the sling and opened his mouth to scream.

Bolan took two quick steps, drew his knife, and then lunged forward. The upswept blade slashed the priest under the chin, cutting off the scream before it left his lips.

The man slumped forward, but Bolan caught him before he hit the floor. Grabbing the hem of the long black robe, he pressed it into the dead man's throat, slowing the blood flow. He dragged the deadweight the length of the sanctuary and opened the curtain to the confessional before dropping the body inside.

The Executioner ripped the cassock from the priest and retraced his steps, wiping the blood from the ancient stone floor. He'd just finished when he heard more footsteps and voices from the hall.

Bolan raced back to the confessional and slipped inside one of the two unoccupied stalls. He heard the men from the hall cross the rock floor. As they neared, the door to the catacombs opened on his side.

Breathing shallow wisps of air, the Executioner listened as two men from the hallway and someone from below met in front of the confessional, conversing in Farsi.

After what seemed like hours in the tiny rectangle, the three men headed back across the sanctuary. Bolan risked a glance through the curtain, seeing them exit into the hall.

Seconds later the Executioner tied the cassock tightly around the dead man's neck wound, then shouldered the body. Ears pricked to every sound, he made his way from the sanctuary and down the hall to the steps leading to the storage room.

In the storage room once more the Executioner paused to catch his breath. With any luck the "priest" wouldn't be missed until tomorrow morning. But as soon as he was, a search of the premises would be launched. Whatever remnants of blood Bolan had missed in the dim lighting of the sanctuary would be discovered.

Still, it might be some time before an all-out alert went into effect. A few bloodstains wouldn't automatically tip the terrorists to a rescue attempt. As long as the body wasn't found.

Three blocks from the Maronite church the Executioner deposited the dead man under the wood-and-concrete rubble of a bombed-out building. He glanced at his watch. Six hours had elapsed since he'd first entered the church.

Sharon Walker was six hours closer to the gallows.

The Executioner kept to the alleys until he neared the small hotel. He glanced at the eastern sky. Dawn would be breaking soon.

The dawn of Sharon Walker's execution day.

14

A shiver of fear surged from Muhibbi's chest down to his legs. He was falling.

The nomad sat upright in bed, his hand fumbling for the .45 on the table beside him. He had thumbed off the safety by the time he realized he'd been asleep. He stood and slipped the .45 into the waistband of his pantaloons, a short tremor of guilt replacing the fear. Walking slowly toward the window, he gazed through the darkness at the church across the street.

Th big man was either alive or dead somewhere inside the stone building.

The nomad still wasn't sure what the true motive had been in demanding that he stay behind. The big American was right, of course. Two men *would* be much easier to detect than one.

But two men provided twice the firepower if they were discovered.

Was he being protected? It didn't seem likely. The nomad knew he had already proved himself as an able fighting man. He wasn't in the same league as the mysterious American, perhaps, but who was?

Didn't the American trust him? If that was the case, then why had he been allowed to continue with the man at all?

Behind him the quiet click of the doorknob thundered like a grenade in the still night. Pivoting on the balls of his feet, Muhibbi drew the .45. Mack Bolan slipped quietly into the room, crossed the floor and sat on the bed.

"They are there?" the nomad asked.

Bolan nodded. "At least some of them."

"You saw them?"

"No, but I know where they are, and I heard them."

Muhibbi listened attentively while the warrior explained what had transpired at the church.

"The police won't find the priest?" he asked.

"Eventually, yes," Bolan replied. "But not tonight. He's several blocks away—minus his cassock and cross. Even if he's found, we'll be out and long gone before they put two and two together and realize who he is."

Muhibbi nodded. He walked to the wooden chair in the corner and unslung his scimitar scabbard from the back rest. Drawing the blade, he ran his thumb lightly up the edge.

"We'll be vastly outgunned," Bolan told him. "You've got your sword and Snodgrass's .45 and extra magazines. I'll use the Eagle and this." He held up the PM-63. "One mag only. I've got four left for the .357. I guess I don't need to tell you we've got to pick up firepower along the way."

Muhibbi slid the scimitar into the scabbard and stuck it through the sash at his waist, fitting the .45 snugly next to it. He glanced up briefly and saw a frown on the American's face.

"This is the last opportunity to back out," Bolan warned. "Are you with me?"

Muhibbi hesitated briefly, then said, "Yes."

Muhibbi followed Bolan down the stairs to the lobby, where the landlord had already set out a breakfast of pita bread, dried fish and coffee. The old man sat in a threadbare armchair, his eyes glued to a morning news report on an ancient black-and-white television.

Both men stopped in their tracks as a familiar face appeared on the screen. Muhibbi watched as a bearded man pressed the blade of a long dagger against the throat of a weeping blond woman. The man's savage eyes glared madly as he shrieked in Farsi.

Muhibbi stood frozen as his own face shouted at him from the screen. Then the picture returned to the newscaster. The nomad turned to Bolan. "This is the tape you saw in America?" he asked.

Bolan nodded solemnly.

"It's my brother."

The big American nodded again. "Last chance. I won't hold it against you."

Muhibbi stared into his companion's eyes. What *was* a brother? Was it no more than the result of the merged loins of mother and father? The man before him had spared his life. Then his heart, his mind, his soul. Now, together, they were about to risk their lives to free innocent people they had never met.

Could mere blood ever transcend the bond that had developed between them? No, Muhibbi suddenly realized. The American was more his brother than the demented, frenzied person he'd seen on the screen could ever be.

Bolan's hard stare seemed to bore holes through the nomad's face. "Are you with me?"

"I'm with you."

He saw the big man's eyes soften slightly. Without speaking the big American turned toward the door, and Muhibbi followed him into the street.

STEADY DROPS of moisture from the overhead stalactite roused Sharon Walker from her sleep, and she sat up on the top bunk. She watched silently as Harun made the rounds of the beds, shoving roughly at the shoulders of the members of Group Two and bringing them to consciousness. He paused at her bed and ran a quick hand from her hip to her thigh.

Still half asleep, Sharon turned and threw her feet over the side of the top bunk. Slowly she descended the rungs of the ladder, feeling the coarseness of the rough wood beneath her bare feet.

As her feet left the ladder and met the cold stone floor, sudden realization snapped her to wakefulness. The day had come. She'd die tonight at midnight.

Strangely Sharon felt nothing as she fell into the bath line behind the banker. She waited silently as the man disrobed behind the sheet Harun held aloft, then dropped over the edge of the floor to the water below. Automatically she turned her head to allow him whatever remnant of dignity he still possessed.

Sharon thought briefly of her husband and two daughters. What time was it in Texas? If it was morning here, it had to be night in the Central Time Zone. Somewhere across the world Don was reading Christie and Amber a bedtime story. Was it yesterday night...or tonight? In her present confusion she couldn't even remember if the U.S. was ten hours ahead, or behind, the Mideast.

If she was still *in* the Mideast.

The banker rose from the water and stepped behind the sheet. Sharon waited until he'd dressed, then moved to the edge of the rock.

Harun held the sheet, leering over the edge as she dropped her pajamas to the floor. She'd turned and bent to enter the water when she felt his hairy hand between her legs.

Without thinking, Sharon Walker wheeled on her feet, brought the palm of her hand around and slapped Harun soundly across the face. He dropped the sheet as the sharp crack of skin against skin echoed throughout the cavern. A fingernail had caught in the guard's nose, and a thin line of blood trickled from his nostril.

Instantly a dozen rifle barrels swung Sharon's way, and she heard the clicks as the men readied their weapons. Suddenly anger replaced the fear and shame that had overwhelmed her for so many months. Standing naked before the guards and other hostages, she screamed toward the cavern ceiling. "Go ahead, you sons of bitches! Kill me! Rape me first, if you want to. I don't care anymore! There's nothing...*nothing* you can do to me that makes any difference now!"

Sharon saw the leader emerge from the mysterious hole in the rock where he so often disappeared. Casually he crossed the cavern. Harun shrank as Darazi stopped next to him.

The Hizbullah leader spoke softly, and Sharon saw Harun shake his head vigorously, then point an accusing finger her way. Darazi nodded and Harun stood straighter, smiling and returning the nod.

Draping an arm around Harun's shoulder, the taller man smiled. He looked at Sharon, said something and both men laughed.

The leader moved between her and Harun and snapped his fingers. Another guard placed a long, curving sword in his hands. Darazi took another step toward her and rested the blade against the side of her neck, as if measuring the angle. His daggerlike eyes bored holes into her skull.

Suddenly the sword shot back over Darazi's shoulder. He turned, whirling away from her, and brought the blade around behind him. The fierce weapon sliced cleanly through Harun's neck near the collarbone.

A thin line of blood trickled from around Harun's neck as the little man's eyes widened and his hands rose to his throat. Then jets of crimson flooded his vest as his mouth gurgled noisily. His head toppled from his shoulders, hit the stone floor and rolled to a stop between Sharon Walker's feet.

As the body fell backward, Sharon realized with a sense of macabre amusement that she felt nothing. She stared at the headless body on the floor in front of her. Slowly the kicking and jerking subsided.

Sharon began to dress as one Hizbullah man lifted the head and two more dragged the body to one of the boats. She followed another guard to her accustomed spot on the rock floor.

Dropping to a seat, she closed her eyes and whispered, "Dear God, forgive me for the sins I have committed throughout my life. Forgive me for... adultery, for sleeping with Randolph Groethe. We... needed each other. We needed... something.

Accept me into your arms and forgive me most for fearing death.''

Sharon opened her eyes, and a new feeling of peace and tranquility came over her.

God had forgiven her.

And she'd forgiven herself.

A guard returned to her side, the familiar black hood in his hands. She looked up and met his eyes. ''No,'' she said firmly.

The guard hesitated, then turned and walked away.

Sharon Walker realized that she wanted to live. She wanted to see Don again, make love to him and watch Christie and Amber grow into women. She wanted to become old, and have grandchildren, and sit by a fire next to her husband and get excited when her family came to visit.

She wanted to eat something besides rice, and do countless other things she'd been deprived of during the past two years of shame, humiliation and dehumanization.

Yes, she wanted to live.

But finally she was prepared to die.

15

Light morning traffic moved along the streets as Bolan and Muhibbi left the hotel. Clouds of dust drifted through the air, fallout from the bombings, burnings and general destruction of the previous day. Walking to the corner, they crossed the street, then cut down the alley.

Bolan glanced toward his companion. Seeing the Hizbullah leader's raving face on the screen just now had explained why Muhibbi had seemed familiar when the Executioner first saw him at the Yazidi camp.

It wasn't Muhibbi's face that he'd seen before, but that of his twin brother.

Over the past two days, the nomad had more than justified the faith the Executioner had placed in him. But Muhibbi would soon face the acid test. The odds were more than even that his brother was inside the church. And while Bolan had no doubt that the nomad would never turn on him, he wondered what reaction Muhibbi might have if conjecture became reality.

Bolan turned to him as they neared the office complex next to the church. "Keep it quiet as long as possible," he whispered.

The man nodded, tapping the hilt of his scimitar.

"We've got to neutralize the ground floor first," Bolan continued. "After we free the hostages, our hands will be full. We can't baby-sit and fight at the same time."

He left Muhibbi behind the office building and dropped into the window well. A moment later the nomad joined him in the dark basement of the church.

The two men crept cautiously around the stacks of boxes and started up the stairs. As they gained the landing, a man carrying a cardboard box turned the corner, coming down. In a second the guy dropped his burden and reached under his vest.

Bolan leaped forward, one hand covering the terrorist's mouth while the other grasped the man's vest and pinned the gun hand against his chest. Pulling hard, the Executioner yanked the guy down into the basement. The man twisted from his grip as Bolan drew his knife. Bolan lunged with the dagger, then stopped short as the blade of Muhibbi's scimitar flashed through the air, sinking into the man's throat.

A voice called from the top of the stairs. "Hamid?" Bolan and Muhibbi dragged the body behind a row of boxes as the voice called again. Then footsteps sounded on the steps.

A moment later a man in an apron, carrying a butcher knife, stepped down into the basement. Bolan sprang from cover, his left arm encircling the man's neck. Pulling the surprised form toward him, the Executioner snapped the terrorist's head back, exposing the jugular vein. After one slashing motion, the man was dead.

Slowly Bolan and Muhibbi ascended the steps. Back to the wall, the Executioner slid along the hallway, away from the sanctuary. At the end of the passage he cracked the swinging door and saw a small kitchen. Two men, one chopping meat with a thick cleaver while the other rinsed the pieces in a large bowl of water.

The Executioner held up two fingers. He pointed at the nomad, then motioned to the left side of the room. Muhibbi nodded.

Bolan burst through the door, Muhibbi at his heels. The two terrorists looked up in astonishment, then the man with the meat cleaver raised it over his head.

The Executioner ducked under the flashing steel and drove a shoulder into the man's sternum, knocking the wind from his lungs as they crashed into the wall. Behind him, he heard a short gasp, then the sound of a body hitting the floor.

As the man with the cleaver rebounded off the wall, the Executioner took a short step back, then thrust his knife through the terrorist's rib cage and into his chest. The cleaver rattled to the floor as the man collapsed into a sitting position against the wall.

Bolan turned to see Muhibbi wiping the blade of his scimitar on a dish towel. He glanced through the door at the rear of the kitchen. It led to a small rectory. The stark room contained only a bed, a portrait of St. Maron on the wall and a portable shortwave radio on the night table next to the telephone.

Quickly Bolan and Muhibbi stripped the bodies and donned their clothes. The Executioner held no false hope that they'd pass for the dead terrorists. But the vests and loose trousers seemed to be Hizbullah's unofficial uniform. The clothes might easily cause a split second of indecision in the minds of the remaining guards. And a split second could make the difference between life and death.

Making their way down the hall, the two men crossed the sanctuary to the door by the dais. At the end of the hall they found several musty classrooms and what appeared to have once been a library.

Bolan had left the door to the catacombs unlocked. Easing it open, they made their way down the stairs to the humid maze below. As they reached the fork in the main tunnel, the Executioner motioned Muhibbi to the left, then grasped his vest as he started to leave. "If you find anything, sit tight," he whispered. "I'll join you as soon as I can."

The nomad nodded and took off through the water.

Bolan waded slowly through the hallway, retracing his steps of the night before. As he neared the first corner, he suddenly heard strange clicking noises accompanying the sound of someone sloshing through the water toward him.

A second later a terrorist wearing rubber thongs and carrying a suppressor-equipped Heckler & Koch MP-5 rounded the corner. He stopped dead in his tracks, a smile crossing his face. Then the corners of his mouth dropped as he focused on Bolan's face. His hand rose to the trigger of the MP-5.

Bolan drove a solid left hook into his face. The gunner splashed backward into the water. Reaching down, the Executioner ripped the subgun's sling over the terrorist's head. As the man started to rise, Bolan snapped his foot out, catching him under the chin. The thongs bounced off the wall into the water as the man fell once more, his head splashing through the water to strike the rock floor beneath. He didn't move again.

His back scraping the rock wall, Bolan edged his way down the final leg of the tunnel. As he neared the spot where he'd heard the woman's sobs, he peered around the corner.

Three armed guards sat on a wooden platform just above the waterline. Seated on the bare wood, ten feet to their right, Bolan saw the disheveled forms of three men and a thin, wrinkled woman in gray pajamas. All four were bound at the wrists and ankles.

The Executioner's thumb found the H&K's safety switch and clicked it to full-auto as he stepped through the door. All three guards started to rise as he squeezed the trigger, stitching figure eights of hushed parabellums back and forth across the terrorists. One man, wearing a black T-shirt under his muslin vest, fell from the platform into the water. The other two collapsed backward, their straight-backed chairs overturning as they fell.

Bolan leaped onto the platform and read the confusion in the eyes of the Americans. An older man, long strands of gray hair falling over his forehead, opened his mouth to scream. Bolan shook his head, pressing a finger against his lips. The man sighed softly and closed his mouth.

The Executioner knelt and began cutting through the leather thongs that bound the woman. "Sharon?"

The woman frowned. "Felicia."

Bolan severed the cords at the old man's wrists. "How many more in the other tunnel?" he asked.

A quizzical expression crossed the old man's face. "We're in a tunnel?"

A blond-haired man in his mid-twenties spoke. "We were wearing hoods when they brought us here, sir."

Bolan turned to him. "Military?"

The young man nodded. "Marines... Security Force."

"Name?"

"Mason, sir."

The Executioner looked into the young man's eyes. He had to have been captured years ago before the troops pulled out of Lebanon. "What kind of shape are you in, Mason?"

"As well as can be expected, sir," came the reply.

Bolan sliced through the thongs at the Marine's wrists and ankles. He jerked his head toward the fallen bodies. "Grab a weapon," he ordered.

The young Marine crawled toward the Uzi.

The Executioner led the frightened Americans down the tunnel. The thin woman gasped as she rounded the corner and saw the body of the man who'd worn the thongs. Bolan put his arm around her shoulders and guided her to the stairs.

"You'll be in the sanctuary when you get to the top," he told the group. "Take the door to your left and follow the hall through the kitchen to the rectory. Wait there until you see me again."

The short, emaciated woman looked up, her eyes full of fear. "But what if we *don't* see you again?"

"Then make your way out as best you can." Bolan turned to Mason. "You'll be in charge."

"I'll go with—"

Bolan cut him off. "No way." He hooked a thumb at the other Americans. "I need you to look after them."

The young man frowned, then turned and led the Americans up the steps.

Starting down the second tunnel, Bolan moved cautiously around each twist and turn, passing the rotten wood of caskets and carved monoliths that decorated his path. Occasionally the main tunnel branched to the sides and he was forced to detour, exploring each crevice before returning to the main route.

As he moved through the winding labyrinth, the Executioner had a sense he was gradually heading west, away from the sea. His hunch was confirmed as the water current beneath his feet slowed, then grew still. Little by little the waterline dropped. As he neared another corner, the dank water ended completely in a stagnant pool.

Bolan stopped abruptly. From around the curve came a sharp, angry shout.

Dropping, prone, he peered around the rock to see a large cavern twenty yards ahead. In the middle of the room eight Hizbullah men surrounded a figure in black pantaloons.

Muhibbi.

A plump terrorist, sweating through his soiled white undershirt, shouted angrily, then pressed the barrel of the .45 into the nomad's neck. Through the mass of arms and legs the Executioner caught glimpses of three huddled men in gray pajamas at the rear of the cavern.

The man in the dirty undershirt turned to a terror-ist with black shoulder-length hair. He barked orders, then pressed the .45 harder into Muhibbi's neck. The long-haired man broke away from the group and jogged toward Bolan.

The Executioner pulled his head back around the corner and rose to a crouch as the running footsteps neared. He sprang as the man rounded the corner. Reaching up, he grasped the long locks of hair in both hands. Redirecting the man's own forward momen-tum, he twirled the terrorist's body in a half circle, guiding the man's head forcefully into the wall, then lowering the limp form to the floor.

Looking around the corner again, Bolan saw the fat man in the undershirt cock the .45, then jam it back against Muhibbi's neck. The warrior flipped the subgun to semiauto, extended the telescopic stock and pressed the butt of the MP-5 against his shoulder. Resting the front sight on the undershirt of the man with the .45, he sighted down the barrel.

Behind the terrorist, directly in the line of fire, sat the gray-clad hostages. The penetrating Winchester hardballs would exit the submachine gun at close to thirteen hundred feet per second. The full-metal jacket would bore straight through the flab beneath the ter-rorist's undershirt and into the seated Americans.

Bolan dropped to one knee, steadying his forward arm against the stone wall. With the sights zeroed in on the man's temple, the line of fire cleared the hos-tages by two feet.

The Executioner steadied the weapon and took a deep breath. Letting half of it out again, he stared through the rear aperture at the front post sight. The shot had to be perfect. The terrorist had to be terminated before his finger could tighten on the trigger and send a half inch of metal through Muhibbi's throat.

As the fat man in the undershirt screamed again in Farsi, the Executioner squeezed the trigger. The warrior felt the light recoil against his shoulder. Still looking through the sights, he saw the fat man's cheek explode. The soft, muffled cough of the sound suppressor slid along the rocks as blood and bone fragments showered Muhibbi and the rest of the guards around him.

Silence filled the catacombs as all eyes turned to Bolan, who jumped to his feet and raced down the corridor. Dropping the MP-5 to the end of the sling, he palmed the big Desert Eagle.

The time for stealth had ended. What he needed now was all the noise and confusion he could generate.

The first booming .357 round punched the man behind Muhibbi in the chest, driving him backward to fall over the seated hostages. Bolan saw the nomad dive for the floor.

Sprinting through the opening into the cavern, the Executioner pounded a double tap of Magnums into the closest man, then hit the floor, rolling to his right as a burly terrorist recovered from shock and raised the barrel of an Uzi toward him. Firing from the ground, Bolan's first slug caught the man in the throat.

From the corner of his eye the Executioner saw two terrorists jerk pistols his way. Turning, he drilled a round through the face of a Hizbullah man with a revolver. The second gunman returned fire with a Browning BDA.

Bolan felt fire skim across his shoulder as one of the slugs burrowed through the material of his jacket and shirt.

Muhibbi somersaulted across the floor and came to a stop next to the man with the Browning. A flash of gleaming metal streaked through the air as the nomad's scimitar swept across the floor like a sickle, severing the gunman's feet at the ankles.

The Hizbullah man lurched forward, catching his balance momentarily on the stubs of his calves. He looked to the floor, his eyes widening in astonishment as he suddenly found himself six inches shorter. Shrieking in agony, he toppled to the floor.

The last two terrorists took off across the cavern, twisting to fire behind them as they attempted to reach another exit on the far side of the cavern. Bolan rose from the ground and started to fire, then stopped as both men ran behind the terrified hostages.

As they cleared the Americans, the Executioner burned a Magnum round through the chest of the lead runner. The man following him jerked as Bolan's second blast tore through his upper arm. He paused, returning fire with an AK-47, then disappeared through the opening into the tunnel.

Bolan turned to Muhibbi, who knelt next to the wounded man on the floor. "Get him bandaged and keep him alive," he said. He glanced toward the hostages. "Cut them loose. But tell them to stay put."

The nomad had anticipated the order and was already wrapping torn strips from the terrorist's vest around the stumps at the end of the man's legs.

Dropping the half-empty magazine from the Desert Eagle, the Executioner rammed a fresh box of .357s into the grip, then returned the big automatic to shoulder leather.

Bolan checked the remained rounds in the MP-5. Six.

Surprise was no longer an advantage. He had no idea what twists and turns this new tunnel would offer for an ambush, and he had to assume that the Hizbullah men would be familiar with every nook and cranny in the deadly, puzzling labyrinth.

But he couldn't allow the fleeing terrorist to alert his comrades of the rescue.

Seven Americans had been freed. Somewhere eight more sat waiting to die.

Among them was Sharon Walker.

The Executioner flipped the safety to full-auto. As he neared the tunnel, he saw blood from the fleeing man's arm wound on the floor before him. Drawing a deep breath, the Executioner headed into the maze.

16

The trail of blood extended down the corridor, the wide red splotches tapering to narrow tips that pointed out the direction of the terrorist's flight. A hundred feet from the cavern the trail led to a small pool before coming to an abrupt halt. Bolan glanced cautiously around and overhead to the casket ledges. His prey had paused here to stop the blood flow.

The man wasn't wounded badly—that was obvious. The impact spatters indicated he was moving too quickly for any serious damage to have occurred.

Bolan moved on warily, his battle senses tuned to the slightest noise, the smallest variance in the monotonous rock walls ahead. Ahead, the Executioner saw a corner and the tunnel branched yet again. Sliding carefully along the rocky wall, he looked around the edge to see a small alcove at the end of the short wing.

Rats scurried around Bolan's feet as he entered the dug-out cavity. More rodents hurried to hiding as he stepped into the alcove. Against the far wall sat the body of a man in a priest's cassock.

Bolan retraced his steps to the main passage. The body explained how Hizbullah had taken possession of the Christian church. It would have been a simple·

enough job to murder the unsuspecting priest, substitute an impostor and tell the congregation that a transfer had taken place. In this war-torn country of religious upheaval, who would have questioned the authenticity of the replacement?

The Executioner moved on, the MP-5 leading the way. He stopped to inspect each monolith, each coffin ledge he passed, checking every recess large enough to conceal a man. For a short distance the blood trail reappeared, then vanished once more.

Bolan rounded a sharp bend and suddenly realized the path had circled, doubling back. He was now headed toward the cavern where Muhibbi waited with the footless terrorist. Passing the tunnel where the priest still lay, he moved on to where the first bloody trail had ended.

He'd carefully checked each possible hiding place as he went, yet the wounded man hadn't appeared. That could mean only one thing. The fleeing Hizbullah man was still ahead, either in or close to the cavern where Muhibbi waited.

The Executioner quickened his pace. Rounding the final curve, he looked ahead to see the wounded man squatting at the entrance to the cavern. His back was to Bolan, and the AK-47 stock pressed against the man's shoulder as he sighted in on some unsuspecting target across the large room.

Without thinking, Bolan raised the MP-5 to his waist and sent three muffled shots into the squatting man. The Executioner sensed a quick flash of movement overhead, and a split second later something heavy landed on his shoulders, driving him to the ground.

A man with a day's growth of beard scrambled onto Bolan's chest, pinning the Executioner's arms to the ground with his knees. Stale breath flowed from behind the five o'clock shadow as he panted down into Bolan's face, at the same time drawing a needle-pointed Qama short sword over his head.

Bolan struggled to free his trapped arms, then rocked to the right, feeling the Hizbullah man's balance break with the movement. As the blade began its descent, the Executioner reversed directions, rolling hard to his left. The eighteen-inch sword scraped his ear as it passed, struck the stone floor and snapped in half.

Bolan rolled farther, freeing his arms, then twisted back to catch the terrorist squarely in the jaw with a back fist. He felt bone shatter beneath his knuckles as the stunned man's head jerked from the impact. Grabbing the terrorist's wrist, Bolan pried away the broken sword before slicing the shortened edge across the man's throat.

Sudden realization struck the Executioner as he rose from the ground. One of the Hizbullah men had to have been out of sight, on the far side of the cavern, when he'd first spotted the men surrounding Muhibbi. When the shooting started, he'd simply slipped down the hall, joining forces with the wounded terrorist somewhere along the way. They'd used the wounded man as bait at the end of the tunnel, while the second man waited to leap from a coffin recess.

They'd been certain Bolan would react to the bait. Their only mistake had been in underestimating how quickly he'd react. A split second slower and the man who'd attacked from above would have landed before the Executioner had fired.

Bolan reached up, feeling his ear. A thin trickle of blood dripped from the scratch. He walked to the fallen man at the cavern entrance, grabbed the sling of the AK-47 and looped it over his head.

"MY WIFE," the bald man in pajamas pleaded as he helped Bolan gather the scattered weapons. "Is Felicia all right?"

Bolan nodded. "She was in another tunnel. She's upstairs now." He tucked another Desert Eagle into his waistband and slung the Uzi over his shoulder next to the AK.

Muhibbi hoisted the footless terrorist onto his back, blood oozing from the crude bandages on the man's ankles as the Executioner led the group through the winding tunnel and up the stairs.

Bolan cracked the door and saw an elderly woman in a black dress and shawl kneeling behind one of the pews. He shook his head. The church had evidently remained open during the Americans' captivity, conducting business as usual while the hostages awaited death in the underground catacombs.

Heaven above, perhaps, but hell below.

The Executioner waited until the woman finished her prayers and rose slowly to her feet. When she'd left the church, he led the hostages through the sanctuary to the rectory.

Tears of joy fell from the eyes of the bald man as he embraced his wife. Bolan gave them a minute, then called them to order. "We're not out yet," he warned. "I want you two to go into the kitchen." He indicated the man and wife. "Pack all the food you can carry." He turned to two of the men. "Scout the church. Find any clothes you can. If you have to, take them off the terrorists."

Bolan looked into the eyes of the young Marine. "Mason, somewhere there's a key to the van parked out back. Find it." The man nodded and left the room.

"The rest of you," the Executioner said, "stand up. Walk around and stretch out. It's not a long trip ahead—but anything can happen."

Bolan looked at the telephone on the nightstand. Chances were good that it was monitored. Leaving Muhibbi in charge, he left the church and crossed the street to the hotel. He'd considered drawing Mason a map and sending them to the Yazidi camp. But that would have involved crossing the border, and there was no way of knowing which Syrian officials might secretly sympathize with Hizbullah. The Americans might find themselves out of the frying pan and into the fire, with the world never learning what had happened.

No, he thought as he entered the lobby, there was a better way—shorter and more secure—to get the hostages to safety.

The Executioner crossed to the desk and set three Lebanese bills on the counter and asked for change. The girl smiled shyly as she traded him a handful of coins.

In the phone booth Bolan closed the folding door behind him and picked up the receiver. Depositing a coin, he waited for the operator. "Amman," he said, then gave an unlisted Company number that would be rerouted several times to connect him eventually to Tel Aviv.

Bolan's mind traveled backward as he waited for the call to be put through. He thought of the raven-haired beauty who'd helped him destroy the Assassins' headquarters on Alamut.

Bolan heard the phone ring on the other end. The number was a safe line that connected to a sound-proof office in Mossad headquarters. Used for a variety of undercover operations, it was what American intelligence operatives referred to as a "hello" number.

But in Tel Aviv they answered, *"Shalom?"*

"Sarah Yariv," Bolan said.

A moment later he heard the authoritative yet feminine voice say, "Yariv."

"I know your end's secure," Bolan began. "I'm not sure about this one."

"Who is this?" came the reply.

"An old friend. We met on a mountain in northern Syria."

There was a long pause at the other end of the line, then the voice softened. "If this is who I think it is, we certainly did. How are things on the mountain?"

The Executioner smiled. Sarah was ninety-nine percent sure it was him. But she was a professional. She demanded total assurance. "The mountain's no longer there," he said. He thought briefly of the Israeli air force strike led by Jack Grimaldi that had put a final end to the centuries of terror that had generated from the mountain.

"That's the right answer," Sarah said. "What can I do for you?"

"I'm sending you a package, Sarah, wrapped in white. It'll arrive from the north in about—" he glanced at his watch "—say an hour and a half."

He heard Sarah take a deep breath on the other end. "Is it what I think it is?"

"Half of it. Have your people ready to accept delivery. Just in case there's any trouble from the return address."

"We'll be on our way in five minutes. Are you making the delivery yourself?"

"Not yet. I'm on my way to pick up the rest of the shipment. Maybe then."

"I hope so. I'd like to see you." There was another long pause. "Be careful."

Bolan hung up.

He crossed the street to the church. It *would* be nice to take a short R and R with Sarah Yariv. Maybe after the rest of the Americans had been freed. Right now the thought of any respite from the battles that lay ahead seemed too remote to even consider.

Bolan returned to the rectory to find that the hostages had changed into a variety of costumes taken from the priest's closet and the dead Hizbullah men. It shouldn't make any difference. The border lay less than forty miles away, due south along the coastal road. There'd be no reason for any of them to be seen outside the van until they reached Israel and the Mossad support that awaited them.

Mason had found the van key in the pocket of one of the guards. He informed Bolan that he'd already started the vehicle and checked the gas tank. The gauge read three-quarters full.

Bolan inspected the Marine who'd quickly taken charge of his fellow hostages. The kid looked odd, to say the least. Above the cassock he'd appropriated, strands of long, uncut blond hair peeked around the inside of a blood-spotted keffiyeh.

But beneath the contradictory costume, the Executioner saw the soul of a warrior, the heart of a young soldier whose pride had never allowed him to desert the faith during his years of captivity.

The Lebanon to Israel run was going to be tough, with enemies at every turn, but the Executioner couldn't afford the luxury of worrying about these people once they were out of sight. All his attention would have to focus on locating and rescuing the remaining Americans.

And knowing that this capable young Marine would be leading the way to Israel would allow him that privilege.

Bolan loaded the hostages into the back of the van and slid the door closed behind them. At the driver's window he leaned into the cab. "I know you can do it, kid," was all the Executioner said.

The Marine swallowed and nodded. "Yes, sir." Bolan turned and walked back to the church. The footless Hizbullah terrorist lay moaning on the bed when Bolan returned to the rectory. He glanced at the bandages on the terrorist's legs. Even with the bleeding slowed it was obvious that the man's remaining time could be measured in minutes. "Sit him up," he told Muhibbi.

When the man had struggled to a sitting position, Bolan leaned in, close to his face, then turned to Muhibbi. "Translate everything I say. Word for word."

Turning back, the Executioner stared into the terrorist's horrified eyes. "I don't have a lot of time," he said, then paused while Muhibbi translated.

The Hizbullah man nodded nervously.

"You're going to tell me what I want to know, and you're going to tell me the first time I ask," Bolan continued. "If you don't, I'm going to turn you over to my friend with the sword." He glanced toward Muhibbi. "And if you think he did a number on your feet, wait till he starts working his way up."

Muhibbi translated, and Bolan saw an expression of true horror cover the pale gray face. The Executioner repeated what Cecile had told him about the daily call, and the twenty-second delay, before the hostages would be automatically executed.

The terrified man listened to Muhibbi, then nodded vigorously. He pointed toward the painting of St. Maron that hung from the wall.

Bolan removed the picture. A shallow depression had been scraped into the plaster below the nail, and an appointment calendar stood upright within the hollow. The warrior handed the book to Muhibbi, then stared back at the terrorist as the nomad thumbed through the pages.

Muhibbi looked up. "The calls aren't made by phone."

Bolan glanced at the two-way radio on the night table.

Muhibbi caught his eye and nodded. "Two calls are made each day," he continued. "But there are ten different VHFs to choose from." He looked at the terrorist and said something in Farsi. The man hesitated, then answered quickly when the nomad's hand slid to his sword. He spoke for several seconds before Muhibbi turned to Bolan.

"It's a simple code, yet not so simple," the nomad said. "They began with the first frequency listed, then move to the second, then third, and so on, on consecutive days. When they reach the end, the rotation returns to the beginning. But all ten frequencies are monitored at the other location. A call on the wrong frequency is as bad as no call at all."

Bolan stared at the man on the bed. "Which frequency are you on today?"

The man understood without a translation. He shrugged, then closed his eyes.

Muhibbi drew his scimitar and placed it between the terrorist's legs, the razor edge turned upward to rest against the man's groin. He spoke again.

The terrified man shook his head, the movement causing his shoulders to jerk.

"When's the first call due?" Bolan asked.

Muhibbi's eyes returned to the calendar. "The first has already been made. This morning at 3:07." The nomad smiled. "You were below in the catacombs when it went out." He glanced back at the calendar and the smile suddenly vanished. He looked quickly at his watch. "The second call is due in less than two minutes."

Bolan tore the calendar from Muhibbi's hand. Above the long list of radio frequencies two times had been entered in Arabic numerals. The first read 3:07. Below it was 11:32. The Executioner stared at his watch. It was almost ll:31.

"We'll have to assume they started the system when they moved from Homs Gap to the church," he told

Muhibbi. "It's a gamble, but it's the only card we've got to play." Quickly he turned the calendar to the first entry, seven days earlier. Returning to the present date, he counted down the frequencies to the seventh entry—151.625.

Bolan tuned in the radio, then looked back at his watch. They were already five seconds late.

He jerked the microphone from the clip attached to the radio and held it to the terrorist's lips. "You say the *right* things," he ordered. Muhibbi translated.

Bolan thumbed the mike button while the man spoke in Farsi. He turned to Muhibbi. Both of the nomad's hands still gripped the scimitar handle, ready to slash upward and geld the terrorist at the first indication of treachery.

Waiting until the terrorist finished, Bolan released the mike. The scratchy sounds of static came over the airwaves, then the microphone on the other end keyed as the return call was given. Muhibbi nodded and smiled.

Bolan dropped the mike back into the slot and returned to face the dying terrorist. "Ask him where the other hostages are being held."

The nomad spoke, and the Hizbullah man's weakened eyes dropped again to the blade poised near his testicles before he answered.

"He doesn't know," Muhibbi said. "Only that it, too, is underground, and the place must be reached by water."

Bolan looked at the next time in the calendar. They'd bought the hostages twelve more hours. The next call wasn't expected until 12:01.

One minute after midnight.

One minute after Sharon Walker's death.

Bolan heard a gasp and turned to the man on the bed. The terrorist's mouth hung open, his sightless eyes fixed in place, unblinking.

There would be no one available to make that early-morning call. The stakes had just been raised. Unless the Executioner located the remaining hostages before midnight, all of the Americans would die.

17

Leon Snodgrass had been transformed. He wore a clean, starched and pressed white shirt; the navy blue club tie was knotted perfectly at the throat; a crisply ironed seersucker sport coat draped from the back of his chair.

Bolan and Muhibbi took seats in front of the desk. The Scotch bottle was no longer in evidence, and the office had a cleaner, fresher smell than the alcoholic fetor that had permeated the room on their previous visit.

Briefly Bolan ran down the events of the morning and night before, then repeated the footless man's sketchy clues concerning the location of the remaining hostages.

Snodgrass frowned, the loose skin of his forehead falling down over the rims of his glasses. "Underground," he mused. "And you get there by water?"

"Right."

"There's no place in Beirut that fits that description," the professor said, "but there are two other possibilities—both close by."

The Executioner looked up at the clock on the wall. "I hope so. If they aren't close by, we're fighting a losing battle already."

"Yes, well," Snodgrass continued, "there's Jeita Cave about ten miles northeast of here. It houses a large underground lake that's fed from the same source as the Nar el Kalb River. Beirut's drinking water comes from there. There's about five miles of underground passageways—one of the largest systems of its type in Asia. I've seen it twice." The old man paused. "And that's exactly what makes me doubt the hostages are being held there."

Muhibbi frowned. "Why?"

"Because he *has* seen it," Bolan said. "It's open to the public?"

Snodgrass nodded. "Right."

"And the other place?"

"North of here, too. Almost to Al Batrun. The Phoenician Cliffs are a series of small hills that rise right out of the Mediterranean. Supposed to be a dozen or so caves that open onto the sea, a few big enough to serve Hizbullah's purposes. There was talk years ago about opening them up to the public, like Jeita. Then the war escalated and the bottom fell out of the tourism business."

Bolan frowned. "It sounds like a decent bet. Are the cliffs government-owned?"

Snodgrass's eyes opened wide, a light bulb evidently flickering in his memory. "No," he said, "they're not." The old man rose from behind the desk and walked to the wall, staring at the photograph of his son.

"When John was killed, I went a little berserk for a while. Like I've told you, I was determined to find those responsible and make them pay." He turned back to Bolan and Muhibbi. "I tried everything,

McKay. To make a long story short, I heard a rumor that a consortium of Iranians had just bought the cliffs."

Snodgrass held up his hand. "I know what you're thinking. But when I looked into it, I found out they had all escaped Iran during the revolution." The old man's face colored slightly. He walked back to the desk and glanced briefly into the wastebasket by his chair. "I was doing some pretty heavyweight drinking at the time. I figured since they were pro-Shah there couldn't be any connection."

Bolan shook his head. "The Ayatollah sent out hundreds of spies in that guise during the takeover. There are still plenty of Iranian terrorists masquerading as exiled businessmen. It gets them where they want to go." He rose, extending his hand across the desk. "Thank you, Doctor. I hope you won't mind letting us use your car a little longer."

Instead of taking his hand, Snodgrass sat back down. "Of course. It's yours as long as you need it. But you'll need a boat to recon the caves," he said. "You could waste days exploring each one on foot."

Bolan nodded. "You happen to have a boat, too?"

The old man smiled. "I do. It's not big, but that's not what you need, anyway. And it won't attract attention. There are two conditions."

The Executioner said nothing.

"I want my son's .45 back."

"Certainly," Muhibbi said. He yanked the Government Model from under his coat and set it on the desk.

"And I'm going with you." Bolan started to protest, but Snodgrass continued. "I know what you're thinking. I'm an old man, and whatever combat experience I had back in the Stone Age has long ago been diluted with alcohol.'' He chuckled briefly. ''All right. I know my limitations. But I haven't had a drink since you two left yesterday, and while these shaky hands may not be able to drop every round in the X-ring anymore, they can damn sure drive a boat and leave the two of you free.''

Bolan glanced at the wastebasket at the side of the desk. The bottle of Scotch set atop a stack of discarded copy paper. It was still half-full. His eyes returned to Snodgrass. ''Okay,'' he said. ''I can understand your feelings, but I want this clear up front. You're with us *only* until we locate the right cave. After that you take off and put as much mileage as you can between yourself and the cliffs. Agreed?''

Snodgrass reached forward and grasped the Executioner's hand. ''Agreed.'' Dropping the hand, the old man slid a desk drawer open and produced a Smith & Wesson Model 19 and a smaller, snub-nosed Chief's Special. He tucked the .357 into his belt, then dropped the tiny .38 into the side pocket of the sport coat. Reaching down, he lifted the .45 from his desk and inspected it briefly, then held it out toward Muhibbi. ''You kill any of the sons of bitches with it?''

Muhibbi shook his head.

Snodgrass inserted his arms into the sleeves of his sport coat, thereby covering the weapons. ''Too bad,'' he said. Then a weary smile covered his face as he glanced back at the photograph on the wall. ''Maybe I will.''

BOLAN SURVEYED the Buccaneer as he stepped on board. The open area behind the rail offered no cover or concealment other than a small four-foot storage cabin at the center of the craft. A lone window was set in the middle of both the port and starboard sides of the cabin, and through the glass, Bolan could see scattered rods, reels and other fishing equipment.

Returning to the Buick, the Executioner opened the trunk and wrapped the captured assault rifles and SMGs in his jacket before carrying them on board and stowing them in the cabin.

He wiped the sweat from his brow as Snodgrass made some minor adjustment to the Chevy inboard/outboard, then yanked the cord and brought the small engine to life. A moment later they cruised out to sea before veering north toward Al Batrun.

The Executioner watched the waves break gently against the Buccaneer's bow as they followed the coastline northward. It seemed as though half of his time during the past few days had been spent backtracking, covering territory he'd already covered. From Turkey to Syria to Tripoli. Then back to Syria to deliver the French hostages to the Yazidis. Then Tripoli again before arriving in Beirut.

Now they were heading north once more. It was frustrating as hell, but Bolan knew that within the restrictions he'd imposed upon the mission—no outside help from either Brognola or Stony Man—it had been the only possible course of action.

Snodgrass broke the silence. "Almost there," he said, and a moment later the Phoenician Cliffs rose along the coastline in the distance.

"Take her out a little farther," Bolan directed. "I want to be far enough away that it won't seem suspicious if we're spotted." He walked toward the cabin and Snodgrass pulled on the tiller, guiding the craft away from the craggy slopes.

Inside the tiny compartment he spotted a scratched and scarred leather binocular case on the bunk next to one of the windows. Lifting two outfitted rods from hooks on the wall, he returned to the deck and cast the unbaited lines over the side.

Bolan reentered the cabin and took a seat on the bunk as they came abreast of the cliffs. He pulled the binoculars from the case and put them to his eyes. Staring at the rugged shoreline through the window, he watched for openings as they trolled slowly through the sea.

Fifteen minutes later Bolan spied the first entrance. The hole opened seaward from the cave, its giant mouth yawning toward the boat. It appeared deserted.

Over the course of the next hour Bolan spotted four more smaller apertures in the rocks. None showed any signs of activity.

"We're nearing the end," Muhibbi said. "What do you want to do?"

The Executioner lowered the binoculars and rubbed his eyes. Snodgrass had said there were a dozen or so caves within the hillside. He'd spotted only five. Either he'd missed the others at this distance or they lay hidden from view within one of the several coves he'd seen.

Bolan walked out to the deck and stared toward shore. He hated to move the boat closer and risk the chance of discovery.

He squinted up at the sun. They had approximately two more hours of daylight, enough time to make two more passes before darkness forced them inland to continue the search.

"Turn her around," the Executioner ordered. "We'll try it again." Returning to the cabin, he stared once more at the hills.

By the time they'd returned to the southern end of the cliffs, three new openings had appeared. But none of the trio of entrances looked any more promising than the ones he'd seen on the first pass.

Snodgrass turned the boat around once more. Darkness had almost fallen as they returned to the north end of the Phoenician Cliffs. Bolan had seen no new caves.

"We can go to shore," Muhibbi suggested. "We'll recon the area on foot."

Bolan shook his head. "We don't have time." He turned to Snodgrass. "We've got to move closer," he said. "The only chance we've got is to move directly in and out of each cove and hope something looks suspicious."

Snodgrass killed the engine. "The only thing that'll look suspicious is us."

Bolan nodded. "But we've got less than six hours left before Sharon Walker falls through the trap. And a minute later they'll realize something's gone wrong at the church when they don't get the radio transmission. They'll either hang or shoot the rest of the hostages. At this point being spotted by the enemy is a chance we'll have to take."

"So what's our plan of attack?" Muhibbi asked.

"We've got to look like we're fishing," Bolan replied. "We'll have to assume that if Hizbullah spots us, the boat will be boarded and searched."

"Yes," Muhibbi said. "But surprise will be on our side, won't it?"

"It will," Bolan agreed. "But gunfire will alert anyone nearby. That means the Americans could be dead before we've even found them. We've got to stash the weapons somewhere and play it by ear. We'll go back for the guns after we've located the right cave."

"If there's time," Muhibbi interjected.

"If there's time," Bolan agreed. "Doc, I want you to sail to those trees." He pointed toward a hollow of buckthorns a mile north behind the beach. "Can you make it back to Beirut on your own?"

Snodgrass stiffened. "I could, but I don't intend to. Our deal was that I stayed with you until we'd located the cave. We haven't done that yet. Besides, with this new approach you'll need me now. It'll be a full-time job for someone to steer around those rocks, and if one of you does it, it means one set of eyes searching for caves instead of two."

Bolan hesitated. The man had a point. Two men searching the dark landscape stood a better chance than one. He hated to expose the professor to the potential danger that lay ahead, but he understood well the old man's desire to avenge his son's murder.

The burning drive to seek justice for the death of a family member was nothing new to the Executioner.

Leon Snodgrass had lost everything after his son's murder. Now he had regained his dignity, knowing that if he couldn't locate the killers, he was at least engaged in a war with their brothers.

"Okay," Bolan told him, "but as soon as we've located the entrance—you're gone. No argument."

Snodgrass smiled. "Agreed. I told you already. I know my limitations." He pulled the rope to the engine and the Chevy choked back to life.

Bolan, Muhibbi and Snodgrass carried the weapons across the beach to the grove of buckthorns, covering the arsenal with a mound of grass and flowers from a nearby field. Quickly the Executioner scanned the deserted coastline. They'd have to gamble that no one would stumble across the weapons before they'd returned to claim them.

Muhibbi kept the scimitar in his sash. Bolan retained only his knife. If they were boarded, assault rifles and submachine guns would give them away in a heartbeat, but Muhibbi's sword wouldn't seem unusual in this war-torn battlefield of the Mideast.

An American with a dagger, however, might raise suspicion, and Bolan decided to stash the knife in the Buccaneer's cabin where it would appear to belong with the boat.

"If we're boarded," Bolan told Muhibbi, "it's up to you. You're a fishing guide, and you've got two American history professors with you."

The sun had fallen from view as they sailed northward, staying as close to the outcropping rocks as they dared. The Executioner poked through the water with one of the fishing rods. The bottom lay somewhere below the five-foot staff, more than enough clearance for the shallow pontoons of the deck boat.

Standing by the outcast lines, Bolan and Muhibbi scanned the dark walls of rock as Snodgrass navigated in and out of the narrow coves. But two hours of close examination yielded no better results than the distant recon they'd undertaken that afternoon.

As they returned from yet another in the seemingly endless series of nooks and crannies, Bolan saw a lone tamarisk tree growing horizontally from a crack in the cliffs. Extending from the apex of a small projection in the cliffs, the tree pointed out toward the open sea. As the Buccaneer glided under the branches, the Executioner estimated they must be halfway back toward the southern end of the outcroppings.

Suddenly the hum of an engine reverberated off the rocks. A moment later a large speedboat appeared in the moonlight, swerving at the last second to avoid a head-on collision with the Buccaneer. The wake of the passing craft hit the deck boat, sending the pontoons scraping against the stony walls of the cliffs.

Bolan heard the speedboat's engine slow to a soft purr. He turned to see the craft spin into a U-turn before gliding slowly toward them. As they neared, the outlines of two forms became visible, and the silhouettes of rifle barrels extended from both pairs of hands.

Bolan and Snodgrass busied themselves with the fishing lines while Muhibbi walked to the edge of the deck. A broad grin covered the nomad's face as the sleek Ranger came alongside.

A young man, his postadolescent beard ragged and sparse, slung an AK-47 over his back, then reached up to grab the rail of the Buccaneer. The driver, half hidden in the darkness, leveled his rifle on the deck as the first man swung on board.

The young man unslung the AK and jammed the barrel into Muhibbi's stomach. He barked a command, and the nomad turned to the two Americans. "Raise your hands over your heads," he translated.

As Bolan and Snodgrass complied, the young man snarled something at the nomad. Muhibbi shrugged and answered, the lopsided grin never leaving his face.

The man at the Ranger's wheel tied his boat to the rail of the Buccaneer, then swung over the side. He walked directly to Bolan.

Moonlight fell on a thin white saber scar extending from eyebrow to nose over the man's swarthy skin. He glared into Bolan's face, then ran his hands around the Executioner's belt line and up and down his legs. Finding nothing, he repeated the procedure with Snodgrass before turning to enter the cabin.

The four men on deck waited silently as the sounds of rummaging emerged from the cabin. A moment later the man with the scar emerged with the knife. Striding purposefully forward, he yanked the scimitar from Muhibbi's sash and held both weapons under the nomad's nose.

Muhibbi shrugged. He pointed toward Beirut, then extended both arms in front of him as if holding a machine gun before jerking them rapidly up and down to simulate recoil.

The man with the scar sneered back at him, tossed the edged weapons onto the deck of the Ranger, then motioned to his partner. Both men swung over the rail and dropped back to their boat.

Muhibbi crossed the deck to Bolan. "They believe the fishing story," he whispered. "And the sword and knife aren't unusual. But we're to leave the area immediately. They'll escort us."

Bolan glanced at his watch. Time was running out—fast. "Do you know where they're going?" he asked Muhibbi.

"Beirut," the nomad answered.

The Executioner fought the curses that threatened to rise from his throat. If they wasted precious time in the company of these two Hizbullah men, the show in the caves could be over before they ever found their seats. One of the men waved impatiently from the Ranger as Snodgrass threw the Buccaneer into gear.

The Executioner turned back to Muhibbi. "Okay," he said. "We'll follow them out of the area. But as soon as we're out of earshot, you follow *me*."

THE BUCCANEER TRAILED the Ranger through the water, the seconds turning to minutes, then an hour as they made their way from the cliffs toward Beirut. Bolan explained his hastily cultivated plan of attack to Muhibbi and Snodgrass as they glided through the dark waves of the Mediterranean.

When the lights of Beirut appeared in the distance, Bolan looked over his shoulder. The cliffs could no longer be seen. They were several miles from the caves and probably out of earshot of any gunfire.

It was the "probably" that worried him. Sound carried well over the sea, the water acting as conduit for even the slightest noise. But if gunfire was heard at this distance, and from the direction of Lebanon's capital, it would be nothing unusual.

The Executioner glanced again at the lights of the city ahead. If they waited much longer, they risked the chance of being overheard on the other end.

The time to strike was now. They'd have to hit hard and fast and hope that any rounds that erupted went unnoticed or were attributed to sources that didn't pertain to the American hostages.

Walking to the rear of the deck, Bolan twisted the Chevy throttle. The congested engine stuttered, then died, the sound of the waves breaking against the pontoons replacing its faint purr. Ahead, he heard the big speedboard engine slow, and the two Hizbullah men looked rearward.

Muhibbi called out in Farsi, and the speedboat circled and came abreast. The youth aimed his assault rifle over the rail and called out what seemed to be a question. Muhibbi pointed at the engine, and at his reply, the man with the patchy beard looked disgustedly at the driver, then leaned his AK-47 against the speedboat. Throwing a line over the Buccaneer's rail, he tied off, then climbed on board the deck boat and followed Muhibbi to the engine.

Bolan moved casually to the rail next to the Ranger. Grasping the cold steel in both hands, he turned toward the men at the engine, watching the driver of the speedboat from the corner of his eye.

When the young terrorist bent to inspect the Chevy, Muhibbi glanced at Bolan. The Executioner nodded. Bolan saw Muhibbi's fist rising overhead as he vaulted the rail.

The man driving the Ranger reacted quickly, reaching for the AK at his side. Bolan hit the deck as the barrel of the Russian assault rifle came down, leveling to line up with his stomach. Still four feet away, the Executioner knew he'd never make it.

Bolan heard a soft click as he lunged across the deck. The safety. In the swift confusion the man with the scar had forgotten to disengage it.

A second click followed the first as the Hizbullah man corrected his error. Bolan dived forward, his shoulder striking the terrorist just below the armpit and knocking the rifle barrel upward.

A short burst flew over the Executioner's shoulder. He stepped back, ripping the AK from the man's grip. Aiming for the temple, he brought the stock around in an arc.

The Hizbullah man turned and the rifle butt smashed solidly against his nose. Stumbling backward, he flipped over the rail and into the sea.

Bolan turned to the deck boat. The young terrorist lay slumped over the engine. His neck extended awkwardly from his shoulders, a jagged shard of pale white bone shining through the broken skin.

Leon Snodgrass lay prostrate on the deck with Muhibbi at his side. Bolan dropped the AK-47 and climbed over the rail. He knelt next to Muhibbi. "A stray round," the nomad explained quietly.

Deep crimson spurted from the dying professor's chest as his open mouth sucked frantically for oxygen. His half-closed eyes rose to meet the Executioner's. "Find them," Snodgrass coughed, more blood spluttering from his lips. "Find them and avenge my son." The old man's chest heaved violently, then his eyes rolled back under the lids.

The Executioner carried Snodgrass's body into the cabin, laid it on the bunk and covered the face with his jacket. Returning to the deck, he motioned to Muhibbi, and both men climbed over the rail to the faster boat.

The nomad kicked the 150 horsepower engine to life. As they picked up speed, Bolan's eyes fell once more on the luminous green hands of his watch.

The time was 10:47. He had a little over an hour to locate the right cave, form a quick plan of attack and rescue the Americans. Seventy-three minutes to carry out Leon Snodgrass's final wish.

18

The armrests of the leather chair were damp with sweat as Mehmed Darazi pushed himself to his feet. In the shadows on the dugout wall he could see the dark forms of Ali and Dawud distributing the evening bowls of rice to the prisoners in the main cavern.

The Hizbullah leader walked through the opening to the brightness of the drop lamps overhead. As always the Americans were seated cross-legged on the floor at the back of the cave. He watched the banker take his bowl, then pick nervously at the rice with his spoon, as did the others.

The Americans appeared to have lost their appetites this evening. Darazi felt a grin break out on his face. It was unfortunate. Tonight was a special night for the hostages. Like children who had no school the next morning, they would be allowed to stay up late. He glanced toward the scaffolding and the new rope that hung from the beam overhead.

And they would even get to watch a show.

"Eat," he urged under his breath. "We will have what you jaded Americans call a 'dinner theater.'" The Hizbullah man threw back his head and laughed with pleasure.

The noise drew the attention of Ali. The tall, muscular man looked up quickly, fear in his eyes, then returned to the business of distributing the bowls.

Ali approached cautiously, his head lowered as he offered Darazi a bowl of the rice. He shook his head, and the underling scampered away.

As Ali and Dawud began collecting the half-eaten bowls of rice, Darazi surveyed the other guards positioned around the cavern. The men dropped their eyes as he glanced their way. All except Dawud, who stared back, a look of revulsion—and perhaps pity—covering his face. The guard shook his head and crossed the cavern with an armload of bowls.

Darazi frowned. He had believed Dawud to be loyal. Now the soul of an infidel bared itself through the traitor's eyes.

Like Harun, Dawud would have to die.

The Hizbullah leader walked to meet him near the boxes of supplies stacked behind the scaffolding. "You are prepared for jihad, my son?" he asked Dawud.

The short man looked up nervously, and Darazi saw that he knew his heart had been exposed. "Yes," Dawud replied, then hurried away.

Darazi followed him with his eyes. Dawud would die. Tonight. Immediately after Sharon Walker. It would serve as an example to the other guards that the penalty for anything short of total commitment was death.

The Hizbullah leader quickly surveyed the stacked boxes of food. They had all the provisions necessary to sustain life for the next few weeks. Still, an hour ago, he'd sent two men to Beirut for a few additional items. The cave entrance would be sealed after tonight's execution. They would isolate themselves and their prisoners as they waited to see what America's response would be.

Darazi leaned against the wooden scaffolding and reached up, tugging gently at the noose that hung through the open trap. Across the cavern he heard a soft gasp, but the Hizbullah leader kept his eyes on the rope.

Who could predict what the Americans might do when they received the next videotape? He could feel the changing tide of jihad growing into a tidal wave, the size of which the world had never seen. In her impotent frustration America might easily choose to bomb Lebanon as they had done Libya.

Good. Such an overreaction would cost the Sons of Satan the few remaining allies who still clung to Mother America's tattered skirts. And it made no difference if the tiny, ineffectual country by the sea was destroyed.

Darazi felt a surge of excitement flow through his veins as he pictured the American war planes overhead, then the bombs dropping through the sky and the destruction that would follow.

Lebanon could be washed into the Mediterranean for all he cared. It would rid his world of hundreds of thousands of the accursed Maronites. And if the country's Islamic residents had to die in the process, that was of no concern, either. Their eyes would open in paradise.

It would be another step up the rungs of the ladder to Allah's Kingdom. Muhammad's Kingdom. *His* Kingdom.

They were all the same. For as Harun's head had fallen from his shoulders to the floor, Allah had provided him with a new vision.

Darazi shouted across the cavern. "Ali!"

The tall man looked up, then hurried to his leader's side.

"Prepare the camera."

Ali scurried into the dugout and returned a moment later carrying the video camera and tripod. Another gasp came from the seated hostages, and then Darazi heard the quiet, sniffling sounds as the American banker wept.

The Hizbullah man studied him with contempt. The weak American pig would be the next to be executed. One week from today.

He scanned the rest of the prisoners, randomly choosing the order of their deaths. His eyes fell on the woman. A twinge of remorse momentarily interrupted his euphoria as he watched Sharon Walker. The sorrow in his breast wasn't for her, but for himself. The pleasure the female body afforded was one of the few glimpses of paradise Allah had granted His children. And Darazi had hoped to glimpse paradise with this woman who had excited him as no other had.

Then she had defiled herself. Darazi's remorse turned to hatred as he recalled the night in the house at Homs Pass. He'd crept silently down the steps to the cellar, determined to take her then, to bring her to his own chamber on the first floor.

From halfway down the stairs he'd seen them, copulating in the damp basement corner like farm animals in heat while the rest of the hostages and the guards slept nearby.

Darazi breathed deeply as Ali set the camera in place on the tripod. Four guards had fallen to his blade that night. He'd considered killing Sharon Walker and her lover, as well, but he knew that the punishment of quick death was too mild an atonement for their sin.

Waiting, with the knowledge of imminent death and the inability of preventing it, was the retribution they deserved, the retribution the American major had already received. And the penalty Sharon Walker was about to pay.

Darazi fought to control his rage as he glared at the woman across the cave. Far in the distance, through the winding passages that led to the sea, he heard the remote sounds of gunfire.

Good. There was more trouble somewhere along the coast, more misery being expressed by his oppressed followers.

He strode purposefully to the dugout, ripped open the top drawer of his desk and produced a videotape. Slowly the Hizbullah leader walked back through the opening and crossed the cavern to Sharon Walker. Squatting in front of the woman, he shoved the tape under her nose. He felt his lips curl downward into a scowl as he raised his arm, then shoved his wristwatch into her face. He took a deep breath as loathing streamed from the woman's eyes.

Leaning closer, Darazi smelled the simple musk of her natural femininity, and the knowledge that he would never possess her heightened his fury.

He had practiced the English words many times in the privacy of the dugout, rehearsing different inflections and enunciations in an attempt to produce a moment of ultimate horror when at last his revenge arrived. Curling his upper lip, he pointed to the face of his watch and said in broken English, "Sharon Walker, you have fifteen minutes to live."

Darazi rose slowly, his anger threatening to overtake him when he saw no response in the woman's eyes. Turning away, he walked to the video camera and inserted the tape. With a last glance at Sharon Walker, he stalked away and disappeared into the dugout.

LESS THAN AN HOUR remained before Sharon Walker and the rest of the Americans would die.

With no time to return to the rifles hidden at the north end of the cliffs, the speedboat cut a furious wake through the Mediterranean as it raced along the shoreline. As the mist pounded against his face, Bolan's eyes dropped to the AK-47 cradled in his arms. He'd searched the Ranger as Muhibbi steered the boat. Besides the knife and Muhibbi's scimitar, he'd found no other weapons or ammunition.

They had the two AKs, one with a partial magazine, the other full. That was it. Not nearly enough, but it would have to do.

Bolan waved to Muhibbi, and the nomad joined him at the steering wheel. "Last chance," the Executioner said. "I can let you out at the edge of the rocks."

Muhibbi stared back at him.

"Mehmed wasn't at the church," Bolan continued. "That leaves only one possibility." He gestured ahead with the AK-47. "Your brother's inside."

Muhibbi's eyes bored holes through the Executioner's. "I'm in until the end."

Bolan slowed the engine as they came abreast of the cliffs, then dropped it to idle as they neared the overhead tree where they'd encountered the two terrorists. Tapping the throttle occasionally for power, he guided the Ranger into the first cove. He circled the inlet as both men strained to detect any sign of activity. Only one small hole, too narrow to admit a man, stared blackly from the rocks in the moonlight.

Returning to the sea, Bolan steered the Ranger around the rocks and into the next tiny estuary. Maneuvering as close as possible to the cliff walls, he studied each crack and crevice. They were heading back out of the cove when the Executioner saw a faint glimmer of light to his left.

Circling again, he guided the Ranger around a massive boulder and through a narrow passageway next to the wall. The light grew brighter as they neared the end.

The Ranger emerged from the tunnel in front of the gaping mouth of a cavern. An oil lamp, suspended with wire, hung from the roof of the cave. Bolan killed the engine and raised the barrel of his AK-47 as the boat drifted toward the opening.

It was little wonder he hadn't spotted the cave from the sea. The cavern entrance opened *away* from the Mediterranean.

Thirty feet inside the passage twisted into a sharp U-turn. Bolan twirled the wheel, steering the boat through the curve. The passageway narrowed, then opened again into an enormous rock room. More lamps hung from the stalactites on the ceiling, casting an eerie yellow glow across the cavern.

Sprouting from the water along one wall of the cave was a series of round wooden posts. A four-by-eight plank ran the length of the shafts, nailed along the tops.

Two boats had been tethered to the plank. The first, a sixteen-foot Lonestar, wobbled at the end of its leash in the soft current. The second, a light fishing boat, swayed harder in the meager swell, jerking against its line and rocking into the Lonestar as the Ranger sent new waves bouncing against the aluminum hull.

Bolan navigated around the two boats toward a tunnel on the far side of the cavern. As they neared the narrowing passage, he heard the Ranger's keel scrape the rock beneath the water.

Without being told, Muhibbi lowered himself over the side. The waterline hit him at the hips, gradually dropping as he splashed toward the tunnel ahead.

The Executioner glanced behind him to the small aluminum craft. The terrorists obviously used the flat-bottomed boat to commute within the inner passages of the cave, switching to the Ranger or the Lonestar when journeying out to sea.

Muhibbi returned and looked up from the water. "We'll take the small boat?" he whispered.

Bolan shook his head and saw a puzzled look wash over the nomad's face. Even the small trolling motor on the aluminum craft would echo down the narrow corridors like a supertanker. The terrorists at the end of the tunnel might assume it was their own men returning, but even so, all eyes would automatically turn their way as they approached. Surprise was the only advantage they had, and the Executioner wasn't about to give it up.

Bolan handed the AKs to Muhibbi, then dropped over the side into the water. Together they pushed the Ranger back to the wooden posts, tying it off next to the Lonestar.

Holding the Russian assault rifle over his head, Bolan led the way down the stony passage. The waterline dropped gradually, then leveled off across his thighs. His eyes fell to the watch on his wrist—11:32. Sharon Walker had twenty-eight minutes.

Bolan heard the hum of a boat motor as he neared a twist in the passageway. Peering around the corner, he saw two men approaching in another of the aluminum boats.

Ducking back around the corner, he turned to Muhibbi and pressed a finger against his lips, then drew his knife. Turning back to the approaching boat, he heard a soft swoosh as the nomad jerked his scimitar from the scabbard.

Pressing his back against the rocks, Bolan crouched low, the knife clenched in an ice-pick grip. He sprang as the boat rounded the corner. Lunging over the side, he slashed downward with the knife, plunging it deep into the chest of the terrorist at the bow. Bolan's other hand reached up, grasped the back of the terrorist's hair. Using the embedded blade and the terrorist's hair for leverage, he hauled himself up and into the boat while propelling the Hizbullah fighter into the water.

The man at the stern rose as the Executioner pulled himself over the side. Bolan's weight rocked the boat forward, then the small craft pitched furiously back, attempting to right itself, before it smashed into the wall of the passageway. The man at the stern toppled from sight into the water.

The boat continued forward, careening off the opposite wall and throwing the Executioner to the metal deck before the motor stalled. Bolan took a moment to snag a SIG-Sauer 9 mm pistol and stick it into his waistband, then rose to his knees and glanced at the water behind him. Neither Muhibbi nor the second terrorist were anywhere to be seen.

A second later a head rose from the water. Then the Hizbullah man fell forward to float on his face, eight inches of blood-streaked carbon steel extending through his back.

Muhibbi appeared next to the man. The nomad rolled the body over and twisted the scimitar with both hands before withdrawing the tightly lodged blade.

Bolan dropped over the side. He saw Muhibbi pull a Tokarev automatic from the body in the water and slide it into his sash.

The Executioner waded to his companion. "They can't be far, now," he whispered. "Stay here."

Muhibbi opened his mouth to protest, but Bolan cut him off.

"I'm going to scout it out. Get the boat ready to move. I'll be back for you."

Muhibbi nodded silently.

Bolan moved on through the tunnel, rounding more curves before hushed voices trailed down the passageway. He dropped to all fours under a lamp, then carefully raised his eyes from the water and peered around the edge of the rocks.

Twenty yards ahead the passage widened into the largest cavern he'd yet encountered. A flat rock floor rose six inches above the water. Roughly a dozen armed men stood positioned around the walls of the cavern. In the center, behind a tripod-mounted video camera, sat eight huddled figures, all dressed in the familiar gray pajamas.

Between the video and a stacked mountain of cardboard boxes a wooden scaffold rose from the floor. Stairs at the side of the gallows led to a platform seven feet from the ground. Suspended from an overhead beam above the platform was a crude noose, dangling at the end of an inch-thick rope.

Two men, Uzis slung from their shoulders, crossed the cavern to the hostages. They reached down and grasped the arms of a blond woman seated near the center of the group.

The Executioner lowered his head, then ducked back around the corner and got to his feet. He glanced at his watch as he ran back toward Muhibbi and the boat—11:56.

Time had run out. Now even the advantage of a surprise approach would have to be sacrificed.

Muhibbi stood by the boat as he sloshed around the corner. "Grab a vest," Bolan said. The nomad vaulted the side and ripped the garment from the man in the boat. Bolan tore the bloody vest from the skewered body in the water and leaped into the boat as Muhibbi choked the motor to life. Donning the vest as they maneuvered toward the cavern, he checked the SIG in his belt, finding a full load and one under the hammer.

Bolan moved to the rear of the small craft, took the tiller and steered the boat around the final turn. Ahead, he saw the two Hizbullah guards leading Sharon Walker up the steps to the hangman's noose above.

The Executioner opened the throttle. The boat swerved slightly, then raced down the final leg of the passage toward the cavern. He saw the shocked faces of the terrorists as they turned to watch the aluminum craft speed toward them.

High on the wooden platform one of the guards dropped the noose around Sharon Walker's neck. The Executioner raised the AK-47 as they left the tunnel and entered the cavern. Tapping the trigger, he sent a lone round searing through the forehead of a man at the edge of the rock floor. The surprised terrorist's eyes widened in disbelief as he toppled into the water.

Bolan stood as they neared the edge of the stone. Four feet from the rock he dropped back to his seat, his two-hundred-plus pound frame sinking the stern as the bow rose from the water.

The light aluminum craft vaulted up onto the rock, both terrorists and hostages scrambling out of the way as the boat skidded across the floor.

Bolan and Muhibbi leaped from the vessel as it ground to a halt in the center of the room. A shotgun blast echoed through the cavern, and Bolan turned to see the first of the guards recovering to return fire. A split second later the roar of gunfire erupted from all sides as the rest of the Hizbullah force entered the battle.

A short burst from the Executioner's AK-47 dropped the man with the shotgun as the high-pitched screams of the hostages pierced through the storm of exploding rounds. Bolan turned to the scaffold, where one of the wild-eyed fanatics reached frantically for the lever to spring the trap.

Sharon Walker's bound and hooded form pressed between the two men as the Executioner raised the AK-47. He thumbed the safety to semiauto and sighted down the barrel, knowing full well that the slightest error in alignment could spell death from his own hand for the American woman. His first round drilled through the lunging terrorist's skull as the man's hand closed around the lever. Slowly the fingers uncurled and the dead man dropped to the ground.

The second man dived across the platform, his arm outstretched. The Executioner squeezed off a follow-up, and the second man flipped from the scaffold to join his partner.

From the corner of his eye Bolan saw Muhibbi drop an Uzi-wielding Hizbullah guard before the nomad's

AK-47 ran dry. Muhibbi drew the Tokarev from his belt as a tempest of fire rained over the Executioner's head.

Bolan dived behind the boat as more gunfire shredded the thin aluminum, sharp slivers of metal embedding themselves in his forearms. Rolling on, he leveled the AK on the man behind the assault and sent a chorus of rounds singing into his lungs.

Two men fell to his side, and Bolan glanced up to see Muhibbi drop the empty Tokarev and dive for the shotgun on the floor. The nomad rose to his knees, racking the slide of the pump gun before blasting a 12-gauge hole through the belly of a terrorist in front of him.

Bolan tapped two short bursts into a duo of guards against the wall, then turned the barrel toward a bearded face firing a Soviet AK-SU through a doorway on the far side of the cavern.

The snarling face glared savagely across the room. Had the Executioner not just seen Muhibbi next to him, it could have been the face of the nomad. Bolan squeezed the trigger, sending a round ricocheting off the rocks before the empty weapon locked open. Mehmed Darazi disappeared behind the rocks.

Dropping the empty AK, the Executioner drew the SIG-Sauer and double-actioned a 9 mm round into the throat of a turbaned man who'd begun to fire at the scattered hostages. He heard the distinctive chatter of a Steyr AUG and turned to see Muhibbi's shoulder explode in a fountain of red. The nomad fell to the floor.

Bolan pivoted, bringing the SIG up in a two-handed combat grip and blasting four 9 mm hornets into the head and chest of the terrorist with the AUG. The man staggered, then slumped to his knees as jets of bright crimson streamed from his wounds.

The last Hizbullah guard continued to return fire from the rear of the cavern. Bolan turned to send two parabellums ripping through his abdomen. The terrorist jerked backward, then raised his Uzi in a final show of force.

The Executioner's next two rounds burned through his head. The final terrorist sank to the floor as Bolan heard the SIG's slide lock open.

Far across the room Bolan saw Darazi bolt through the doorway and race toward the stairs of the scaffold. Dropping the empty SIG, Bolan drew his knife as he sprinted after the man.

Hurdling bodies as he ran, the Executioner strained to reach the scaffold as Darazi's churning legs ascended the steps. He glanced upward at the platform.

Sharon Walker, her hands bound with adhesive tape, the noose still knotted tightly under the black hood covering her head, stood helpless at the top of the stairs. Still ten feet away, Bolan saw Darazi reach the top and lunge for the lever.

Bolan's arms shot up. Catching himself on the overhead platform to slow his momentum, he ducked under the scaffold as the trap flew open.

A high-pitched scream echoed throughout the cavern as Sharon Walker fell. Both of the woman's feet hit Bolan's shoulders, one leg skidding down his chest while the other slid behind his back. The Executioner reached up and caught the screaming woman at the hips. Sharon Walker came to rest in a sitting position on his left shoulder.

Bolan heard the footsteps at the top of the stairs, then Darazi's descending feet appeared through the open slats. The Executioner's eyes turned upward as he stretched to raise his knife overhead.

The rope swayed above him, dangling through the open trap to loop below the woman's collarbone before curving upward again to her neck.

Three inches above his blade.

Bolan reached behind the woman, severed the tape at her wrists and pressed the knife into her hand. "Reach up," he whispered. "Cut it—quick."

Sharon Walker took the knife, wobbling slightly as Darazi reached the bottom step. Bolan felt a jerk as she sliced through the rope. He shifted his feet for balance, then lowered her to the floor.

He looked up into the bore of a Sokolovsky Automaster. Darazi stood ten feet away, just out of reach, in front of the scaffold. A snarling, distorted caricature of Muhibbi, the Hizbullah leader glared at Bolan from above the .45.

Then the features twisted into a sneer as Darazi jerked his head toward the bodies on the floor. "You have accomplished nothing, Satanic pig," he spit. "She is about to die. *You* will watch. Then, before I send you to the fires of hell, I will allow you to witness the deaths of the rest of the American swine." His head jerked again, indicating the gray-clad hostages huddled together in a corner across the cavern.

Darazi aimed the Sokolovsky at Sharon Walker. Behind the Hizbullah leader Bolan saw a blood-soaked form crawl across the floor and pull something from the belt of a dead terrorist, then hide it behind his back.

"Mehmed," a weak voice called as the bloody figure rose to his knees.

The Hizbullah leader turned slightly, the .45 still trained on the woman.

"Mehmed, I am your brother..."

Darazi's deranged eyes filled with shock as he turned toward the voice and stared into the carbon copy of himself. "Muhibbi? It is you?"

The Executioner lunged forward as Muhibbi pulled a Browning Hi-Power from behind his back and pulled the trigger. The round skimmed Darazi's vest, flying harmlessly past both men as Bolan drove his shoulder into the madman's back and reached around to grasp the gun hand at the wrist. A white froth of saliva bubbled from Darazi's lips as Bolan brought a knee up into his groin, then wrestled him to the floor.

"Jihad is here!" the fanatic screamed as he hit the ground, still clutching the Sokolovsky tightly. Bolan forced the gun aside as the terrorist jerked the trigger, sending a wild shot ricocheting around the walls of the cavern.

Bringing both hands to the gun, the Executioner twisted Darazi's wrist inward and jammed the barrel

of the Sokolovsky into the terrorist's mouth. A .45-
caliber concussion echoed throughout the cavern as
the Executioner rose to his feet. He turned and walked
to the woman on the floor. Reaching down, he removed the black hood.

EPILOGUE

Mack Bolan leaned forward, switched on the television and sat back on the bed. A collage of news footage stills flashed across the screen. Above the music an unseen voice quoted chopped sentences from past stories.

"... over two tons of cocaine were seized ..."

"... police stormed the building ..."

"... the young caller explained that his mother and father had been fighting ..."

The music stopped and the voice said, "You get it first on Channel Five—Action News—Detroit."

As the newscast changed to a commercial, Bolan opened the suitcase next to him. He lifted the folded, skeletal frame of a Springfield Armory M-6 Scout and flipped the catch, straightening the weapon. From the storage compartment at the top of the buttstock he removed one CCI CB .22 rimfire.

Bolan opened the weapon's bolt and slid the round into the chamber. He stood and dragged the desk chair across the room to the window.

The low-velocity .22 would leave the rifle at scarcely over seven hundred feet per second, negating further need of sound suppression. The near-silent cough the twenty-nine-grain bullet would produce had been the reason the Executioner had opted for the weapon.

Bolan stared across the street at the restaurant entrance. The hushed .22 was all he needed at this range. The blood would be minimal, and he'd likely be on his way out the door before anyone even realized that a shot had been fired.

He checked his watch. Val Santino was a creature of habit. He arrived like a well-wound clock at the same time every night. The Executioner had ten more minutes.

Bolan leaned the weapon against the wall and returned to the bed. He watched footage of a 747 landing, then Sharon Walker and fourteen other Americans came running down the ramp. Sharon embraced a man holding a yellow ribbon while two young girls in white anklets jumped up and down, impatiently waiting their turn.

The newswoman returned, then Bolan saw scenes from the captured Hizbullah video. Sharon Walker, hooded and trembling, stood once again on the scaffold as a terrorist slipped the noose around her neck. Then the guard's shocked eyes turned from the camera and his hand fell to the weapon on his hip. A split second later the video showed him falling from the platform.

As soon as they'd reached Israel, Bolan and Sarah Yariv had carefully edited the tape, removing all frames in which his face could be recognized. He smiled slightly, remembering the two-day furlough he'd allowed himself once the Americans were safe in the hands of the Israelis.

On the screen Bolan saw Darazi run up the steps of the scaffold and thought of the man's brother. Muhibbi was recovering quickly from the shoulder wound. Already, the nomad was planning to return to the Yazidis and help lead them into the twentieth century.

Bolan moved back to the window and lifted the M-6 as the mafioso triggerman's black Cadillac passed by and parked down the street. Santino exited the vehicle and walked nonchalantly toward the front entrance.

The Executioner opened the window. In the background he heard the voice of the newswoman. "The identity of the man behind the daring rescue is still unknown. Congress is conducting a full investigation...."

The Executioner rested the barrel of the M-6 over the back of the chair and aimed through the window. He'd come full circle in the past week, leaving this same motel room less than an hour before Santino arrived. Now it was time to finish what he'd started before all hell had broken loose in Lebanon.

Bolan pressed the stock against his shoulder as Santino stopped to shake hands with the doorman. Resting the front sight on the hit man's temple, the Executioner squeezed the trigger. Then he rose from the chair and refolded the rifle as the doorman knelt over the body.

The Executioner dropped the folded rifle into the suitcase. He held no illusion that the rescue of the fifteen Americans meant the end of his lifelong war. The war was far from over. More battles remained to be fought. Anyone who doubted that had only to turn on the television.

Bolan reached toward the Off switch as the beaming face of a nurse in a three-cornered hat said, "At Detroit General Hospital our goal is a pain-free world."

"Mine, too," the Executioner told her, and switched off the power.

Bolan's on a one-man mission to avert international disaster
when a group of Irish terrorists plan the unthinkable . . . the
assassination of the queen.

DON PENDLETON's

MACK BOLAN.

BLOCKADE

The Curran Brigade—a new faction of Irish freedom fighters—are
actually ruthless terrorists using patriotism as a front for their
diabolical plans. It's up to Mack Bolan to stop the madness before the horrifying conspiracy is realized . . . and puts the world
at war.

**In the Deathlands,
everyone and everything is fair game,
but only the strongest survive....**

JAMES AXLER
DEATH
LANDS®
Latitude Zero

Heading west toward the nearest gateway, Ryan Cawdor and his band
of post-holocaust survivors are trapped in a nightmare when a deal
necessary for their survival pits them against Ryan's oldest enemy—a
sadistic, ruthless man who would stop at nothing to get his hands on
Ryan Cawdor.